SPECIAL MESSAGE TO READERS

This book is published under the auspices of

THE ULVERSCROFT FOUNDATION

(registered charity No. 264873 UK)

Established in 1972 to provide funds for research, diagnosis and treatment of eye diseases. Examples of contributions made are: —

A Children's Assessment Unit at Moorfield's Hospital, London.

•

Twin operating theatres at the Western Ophthalmic Hospital, London.

•

A Chair of Ophthalmology at the Royal Australian College of Ophthalmologists.

•

The Ulverscroft Children's Eye Unit at the Great Ormond Street Hospital For Sick Child London.

You can help further the work of the Fo by making a donation or leaving a leg contribution, no matter how small, is with gratitude. Please write for d

THE ULVERSCROFT FOUND
The Green, Bradgate Road, A
Leicester LE7 7FU, Engl
Telephone: (0116) 236 4

In Australia write to
THE ULVERSCROFT FOUN
c/o The Royal Australian and Ne
College of Ophthalmologi
94-98 Chalmers Street, Surry
N.S.W. 2010, Australia

FLASHPOINT

Gordon Drew's return to his home town coincides with a baffling series of fires and murders. Drew finds himself secretary to a Dr. Carruthers, an eccentric scientist and investigator, who helps the police solve the mystery of the fires. Meanwhile, Superintendent Denning's methodical investigations lead him to the arsonist. However, when he also discovers a ruthless murderer who exploits science to dazzling effect in his crimes, it is Dr. Carruthers who excels and helps Denning bring justice to the criminal.

Books by John Russell Fearn
in the Linford Mystery Library:

THE TATTOO MURDERS
VISION SINISTER
THE SILVERED CAGE
WITHIN THAT ROOM!
REFLECTED GLORY
THE CRIMSON RAMBLER
SHATTERING GLASS
THE MAN WHO WAS NOT
ROBBERY WITHOUT VIOLENCE
DEADLINE
ACCOUNT SETTLED
STRANGER IN OUR MIDST
WHAT HAPPENED TO HAMMOND?
THE GLOWING MAN
FRAMED IN GUILT

JOHN RUSSELL FEARN

FLASHPOINT

Complete and Unabridged

LINFORD
Leicester

First published in Great Britain

First Linford Edition
published 2007

British Library CIP Data

Fearn, John Russell, *1908 – 1960*
Flashpoint.—Large print ed.—
Linford mystery library
1. Detective and mystery stories
2. Large type books
I. Title
823.9′12 [F]

ISBN 978–1–84617–676–0

Published by
F. A. Thorpe (Publishing)
Anstey, Leicestershire

Set by Words & Graphics Ltd.
Anstey, Leicestershire
Printed and bound in Great Britain by
T. J. International Ltd., Padstow, Cornwall

This book is printed on acid-free paper

1

The young man stood surveying the town interestedly. It was four o'clock in the afternoon, and though a bleak February wind set papers scurrying and made breath visible there was brilliant sunlight.

At the base of the long station slope was spread the multi-coloured patchwork of Halingford, one of many small southern towns and overridden by that Georgian aspect common to most of them. It gave a suggestion of timelessness, of things unmoved . . . or even of stagnation.

At the termination of its descent the slope became Halingford Road, the main street through the town. From it branched the smaller roads leading into the residential areas.

From a town-planning angle it was well arranged — the neat modern villas being on the outskirts and the more stodgy Georgian residences skirting the centre in a rough circle. In the centre itself loomed what industry the town possessed — small shops, with an outcropping of modernism here and there in the shape of a taller, whiter building or the imitation granite façade of a cinema.

Gordon Drew smiled. Nothing had changed in the eight years in which he had been away — except his own fortunes, and for that he had only himself to thank. Hands deep in the pockets of his heavy overcoat, he began walking down the slope.

Everywhere there were interesting things that revived old memories. Mrs. Gabin's sweet-shop was still there . . . He wondered if she were still alive . . . And old Cranborne. And . . . He reached the main street in the town centre. Seeing a familiar small teashop, he turned into it. To his silent disappointment a new proprietor was now in charge.

''Afternoon, sir.'

'I'd like some tea,' Gordon said, and sat down at one of the glass-topped window tables. 'And some biscuits.'

The filled teacup and biscuits before

him, Gordon glanced up. The proprietor took in the details of his customer's face. It was lean, powerful, with a cleft chin. The nose stopped short and the grey eyes seemed both tired and amused at the same time. The hair was black, in aimless little curls, thinning at the temples. One unexpected feature drew the proprietor's gaze — a scar, shaped like a sickle, curved from the man's right ear to a point just below his nostril. It was the kind of scar a severe burn might inflict.

'Thanks,' Gordon acknowledged. 'It's eight years since I left this town. How long have you been here?'

'Six.' The proprietor was not over-informative.

Gordon drank his tea and asked: 'Know a family around here called Lloyd? They used to have a Georgian house with a pillared portico, in Elm Avenue — '

'Sure! Geoffrey Lloyd is the Borough Surveyor. Pretty popular with the Council.'

'When I left he was an architect on his own account. Hasn't he a daughter?'

'Uh-huh — Janice. In the local paper a

lot, giving do's.' The proprietor turned away to attend to another customer.

Finishing his refreshment, Gordon gazed absently through the net-curtained window. Occupying all the corner formed by the High Street and right-angled side road, was Granwell's Emporium. It was one of the newer buildings, unfamiliar to Drew, a storey higher than its neighbours.

He gazed in a leftward direction along the block of familiar shops facing him, finished at Bilkin's fish and fruit store. It was closed now, with a view of imitation marble slabs, empty, visible behind the exceptionally broad double-sash windows.

Drew wondered if old 'Ozzy' Bilkin still ran the place. He'd been a real character in his way. Then there had been little Edith Bilkin, something of a tomboy, he remembered. Eight years ago! That must make her a young woman now, if she were still around . . .

'The emporium's pretty recent, isn't it?'

The proprietor stirred from behind the counter. 'Built about two years,' he answered. 'Granwell's a councillor . . . 'ell of a big pot in his own estimation. Always saying he wished he had a bigger place.'

'Mmmm . . . And old Bilkin? He still alive?'

'The fishmonger? Yes, I see him most days. He buys his bread and cakes from me.'

'And his daughter Edith? Grown up, I suppose?'

'She'll be about twenty. Helps in the shop and on the delivery rounds. From what I've noticed she's going out regular with a chap from the laundry.'

'Very intriguing,' Drew commented dryly, and the proprietor was too obtuse to detect the sarcasm. In fact he was wondering who this young man with the scarred face was, and why he wanted to know so much.

Cultured voice, good clothing, but he had an aloof air that did not appeal to the teashop proprietor. He preferred his customers to be earthy and entirely on his own level.

'Anything else new about here?' Gordon questioned after a pause.

'New? Not as I know of — oh, 'cept for my next-door neighbour. He only came and took over a year ago. Bedford, the florist . . . I think,' the proprietor added, in sour disapproval, 'that he's something of a 'sissy'.'

Gordon got to his feet and fished coins from his pocket with which to pay his bill. 'Oh, I don't know . . . Wreaths are needed sometimes when you die, remember.'

'When *I* die,' the proprietor said, thumping the cash register, 'it'll be no flowers by request. They're silly on a man . . . even if he is a corpse.'

'Keep the change,' Gordon said easily, as at the till drawer flew open with a sharp ring. 'And thanks for the tea. The biscuits need crisping up, otherwise no complaints.'

Leaving the shop he turned up his coat collar against the freezing wind, passed a hand over his disordered, uncovered hair, and then looked in the florist's next door.

A 'sissy' Cornelius Bedford might be, but his offerings were both exquisite and varied. There were daffodils, ornate bowls full of spring violets, queer ice-plants, old-fashioned aspidistras — for ornamentation only — somewhat latent chrysanthemums, carnations and at the back of the jungle a green-painted trellis carrying the decorous statement — 'Wreaths Made to Order'.

Gordon moved on again, intending to look through the glass doorway at the interior, but he found the view blocked by numberless seed packets that formed a positive blind.

Against the inner wall of the entrance-way outside the door was a wrought-iron stand containing three fairly large plant-pots in which reared prosaic-looking cacti.

'Used to be a bicycle shop,' Gordon murmured to himself, then, in an effort to get his bearings, he looked across the road. To the left was the fishmonger's, to the right the emporium. The florist's was midway between the two, on the opposite side of the street, forming the apex of a triangle.

He pensively surveyed the fish and fruit shop. Dimly in the background of the store he could see a large woman moving and stooping. Probably Mrs. Bilkin. He played with the idea of going across and having a chat with her, then he changed his mind and instead began walking up the street towards the centre of Haling-ford.

Ten minutes would bring him to Elm Avenue and the home of Geoffrey Lloyd, now the Borough Surveyor. He had no desire to see the sober-sided, fiftyish Borough Surveyor — but he did have a daughter who, eight years previously, had been a highly delectable schoolgirl, complete with all the attributes that many senior schoolgirls have.

'If at twenty-four she's anything like she was at sixteen, she's well worth a visit,' Gordon muttered, as he strode along. 'Be a surprise for her, too, my dropping out of nowhere like this.'

He wondered what he would say to Janice, how to begin conversation after a gap of eight years. The laws of chance, however — or whatever laws they are which play monkey tricks with us poor humans — were working overtime for Gordon Drew.

A placard inside the grimy window of a shop caught his eye as he passed. At first it did not register, then, catching sight of the name ' . . . Lloyd' at the bottom of the card he went back to make sure.

A social sale-of-work was being advertised, taking place this Monday afternoon — *inside*, with Miss Janice Lloyd as organizer. 'Well,' Gordon breathed, grinning, 'think of that!' He squinted through the steamed window.

Beyond the barrier were the barren shelves of an obviously unstocked shop, while from the ceiling two unshielded electric bulbs hung like stars with haloes around them. He could faintly discern the movement of people in an atmosphere of steamy warmth — and nothing more.

It took him only seconds to make up his mind, then he was within a huge, busy room which was apparently the shop and living quarters all combined in one, the dividing wall having been knocked down.

Along the centre of the room were long tables loaded with a miscellany of objects ranging from rompers to tins of paint, and over them men and women, mostly elderly, needy, and surprisingly genteel, were hovering in curiosity.

Gordon felt embarrassed, as the doorbell clanged over his head and drew unwanted attention. He was too well dressed for this sort of affair, and, if it came to that, perhaps too well nourished.

He forgot all about his self-consciousness as across an outcropping of women's hats he caught a glimpse of a slender young woman seated at a table, busily writing. She was not a senior schoolgirl but her hair was still coppery-red and she had retained that unconscious habit of pausing now and again to pensively stroke her left eyebrow.

It was undoubtedly the same girl who at one time had carelessly swung a schoolbag and threatened to clip the wings of all girls — and boys too — who dared to disagree with her. Independent, forthright, she had been, but at this moment it appeared as though the quality had not survived her adolescence.

Gordon edged between the rooting, critical, murmuring men and women and stopped at the table where the girl was seated. It was covered with papers and correspondence. The girl seemed to have saddled herself with a huge amount of work.

'Hello,' Gordon said, in his easy voice.

The girl glanced up at the speaker, and gave a visible start.

She was less plump than she had been at sixteen, Gordon noticed. Keen, decisive features and firm chin and mouth. She looked business-like, right down to the neat heather-mixture two-piece she was wearing. An emerald-green silk scarf at her throat was in vivid relief to the copper of her hair.

'Gordon Drew!' she exclaimed finally, delight in her blue eyes. 'Of all people! Great heavens, you're not one of the poor and needy?'

'Mebbe,' Gordon shrugged. 'But at least I haven't got to the place yet where I need a cast-off overcoat . . . Gosh, but it's grand seeing you again!' he enthused, shaking her hand warmly. 'How have you been all these years?'

'I should think that's a question for *you* to answer, not me. Where have you been keeping yourself all this time?'

Gordon hooked his foot round a nearby chair and dragged it forward. He sat down beside the girl and grinned at her amiably.

Her eyes travelled unconsciously to the sickle-shaped burn scar disfiguring his face and a momentary frown crossed her brow. Drew sensed the unspoken question but he did not answer it.

'I've been spending myself up,' he explained, sighing. 'Just goes to show — if you don't bring up a child to understand the value of money it brings disaster in the long run. Not that I'm worried. I'll get by somehow.'

She turned away from him for a while to take the money for a man's trilby hat; then again she was studying him thoughtfully.

'I thought you'd gone abroad,' she said. 'Never having had any letters from you.'

'I'm a rotten letter writer,' he said uncomfortably.

'When last we met you told me that your people were selling up that grand house of yours in Sundale Avenue, and moving to London. What happened then?'

'Oh, we went to London all right.' Gordon smiled grimly. 'Then eventually Father caught pneumonia and died within four days. Mother seemed to go all to pieces after he'd gone and wasn't long following . . . That will be three years ago this May. All the money came to me and I went into business.' He gave a forlorn laugh. 'Business! Ye gods! Do you know, Jan, I don't think there could be a worse businessman anywhere. I had a partner — a real slick city gentleman — and I believed everything he told me. I was only twenty-five at the time, and I got taken for a sucker.

'Anyway,' he concluded, 'the project failed. I tried another, and that failed too . . . But why go on? Right now all I have in the world is a few hundred pounds and the clothes I'm wearing.'

'And your father was one of the richest men in this town,' Janice exclaimed, clearly sympathetic. 'A first-class business man too. Remember how he used to do a lot of architectural deals with my father?

And now it's all gone?'

'Uh-huh.' Gordon grinned ruefully. 'I'm still young, though; I've knocked about a bit and learned sense. I'm prepared to work for the first person who'll have me.'

'In Halingford here?'

'I'll probably try London. I've been playing around in different parts of the country and I thought that on my way to London I'd drop in here to see the old places. And to be perfectly truthful I was smitten with an urge to see you again. I wanted to find out if you had become any different from the schoolgirl I used to know — if you'd married. Remember how you cheeked everybody and stood up for the underdog? Well, as I say, I decided to find you — which by chance I seem to have done pretty quickly — take a look at my old home and revive a few memories, then carry on to London this evening.'

'Oh . . . ' Janet hesitated. Stories of adversity always worried her, made draughts in the sheltered, influential atmosphere in which she had her being. It made her anxious to help. She was simply that sort of a girl, a champion of the underdog.

'So there it is,' Gordon said. 'I'm glad you're doing well — or at least your father is. He always was go-ahead, or so my father used to say.'

'Yes, he's made progress,' Janice admitted.

'As for you,' Gordon said, 'you've blossomed out from the sixth-form girl I used to know . . . We had some fun in those days, eh? Picnics, tennis, and — things. I've thought about you a lot in the intervening time. What do you do now — just this social work?'

'I do all sorts of things. There's plenty for a girl like me to do, helping folks. It's surprising what a lot of poverty there is, and a lot of it avoidable, even in a town like Halingford. I do a lot of organizing for social welfares and things. Fills the time in . . .' She changed the subject abruptly. 'Your old home, you say?'

Gordon nodded.

'A funny old codger has it now,' she said, with a faintly puzzled smile. 'Your father sold it to a tea merchant, name of Dodd, didn't he?'

'That's right.'

'Well, he died. Then a Dr. Carruthers bought it. I can't make out whether he's downright rude, absentminded, or just plain crazy. Occasionally I see him knocking about the town, but mostly he seems to keep to himself. I'm telling you this, Gordon, in case you decide to have a look at your old home. Dr. Carruthers is just the kind of man to come out and ask you what the dickens you mean by it.'

Gordon grinned. 'I've no intention of invading his domain. I just want to look at the place from the outside and sort of try and cure my homesickness . . . You know how it is.'

'Well, I . . . ' Janice looked vaguely uneasy. 'Nostalgia's one complaint I've never contracted . . . I suppose you *have* to go to London for a job? It seems a pity to renew our friendship after a gap of eight years and then break it again.'

Janice was clearly hedging, then abruptly she came into the open. 'Why don't you let me ask Dad if he can fix you up in the municipal offices?'

Gordon shook his head. 'I appreciate the suggestion, Jan, but I'm just not the type for filling in forms or obeying routine of any sort — coming and going at regular hours. I think I should gradually go stark crazy. Come to think of it, I'm probably not far from that state now, otherwise I wouldn't be in such a financial mess. However, I've got to have something exciting, unexpected. It's the only thing that keeps me alive.'

'And where's that policy got you? Hardly any money and your future in mid-air!'

Gordon smiled at her, and she was thankful that she had her emotions sufficiently schooled to prevent blushing. But she was aware of a profoundly disturbing element. Men, in the general run, did not interest her in the slightest — but this was decidedly different. Gordon Drew had revived in her mind dozens of old remembrances and half-forgotten promises to herself.

At sixteen, viewing the world through rose-tinted romantic spectacles, she had made up her mind to marry Gordon. Then he had disappeared . . . Now he was back, and around her there were now gathered all the weapons of a mature woman.

'You should settle down,' she said calmly.

'Can't see why at twenty-eight,' Gordon responded, reflecting. 'I want a job that's ticklish, interesting, and off the beaten track — and it's unlikely Halingford can provide that. I certainly can't imagine work in the municipal offices being wildly exciting.'

'But at least it's steady. Regular salary, time to plan properly . . . '

Gordon got up slowly. 'We've outlooks which can't be reconciled, Jan,' he said quietly. 'Just as eight years ago I always dashed across the level crossing as the gates were closing, whereas you waited until the train had passed. It's still that way . . . But it's been grand seeing you.'

'Then — you're really going?' He could see she was fighting to think of some pretext to still detain him.

'For both our sakes,' he answered, and gripped her hand. Then, before her wits could seize upon some new excuse, he had turned and was making his way amidst the moving, murmuring people.

2

Granwell's Emporium filled a much-felt need in the town of Halingford. For many years, the small chemists, booksellers, photographers, stationers, and furniture dealers had had things too much their own way, thriving financially on the fact that their customers had either to pay the prices or else travel to Werton, the next town, where with fares or petrol costs added the price would equal those of Halingford anyway.

Accordingly the Halingford residents had just been forced to pay up. Complaints through the *Halingford Gazette* or to the Town Council had made no impression, chiefly because the paper was partly financed by the councillors themselves and they, in turn, so devised it that they obtained a percentage of all shop profits.

Rupert Granwell with his chain-store mind and financial acumen had stopped all that. Nobody knew where he had come from; there was some cloudy talk about him having come from up north, but wherever his native heath he had certainly made use of the corner patch of soil and brick ends on which the emporium now stood.

And as the giant had grown and been filled with everyday requirements, so had the small shops cowered in disturbed anticipation of events to come. Colossus was in their midst. Granwell's Emporium was now the hub of commodities around which the life of Halingford revolved. If there was a wanted article absent from the stock, it was always promptly obtained, and offered at cut price.

Of Rupert Granwell himself little was seen — or known. Certainly he was a councillor and as such moved in the somewhat rarefied atmosphere of his fellow councillors, only drawing attention to himself in the Council chamber during one of those heated and somewhat Gilbertian debates that are a joy to the local paper.

One particular topic upon which he could always be relied upon to expound vigorously concerned a perpetual land lease, which lease could only be abrogated by Act of Parliament. Nobody seemed to quite understand what he was talking about — the Halingford denizens least of all — but the legal phrases and fiery speeches made grand copy for the local reporters.

Another of his favourite lines was that his one aim in life was to expand his business and — presumably — enrich himself.

Otherwise, visions of Granwell were as rare as total solar eclipses, but those who had looked upon the Presence averred that he was short, stout, pink-faced, with a woolly mat of dark brown hair. He was, it seemed, a man of clipped speech and inescapable authority. The fact that he knew how to handle money, and make it, enshrined him in a position almost deific amongst the none-too-imaginative people of Halingford.

From his employees however, there came a somewhat different story.

Apart from the natural tendency of an employee to regard the Boss as a swine, it was agreed by every one of his five hundred workers that he was a tough nut to work for. He paid well because he was businessman enough to respect the unions — but this did not prevent him getting his pound of flesh. He devised all kinds of involved systems for getting the utmost out of an employee in the given hours of work, systems far too numerous to be classified.

His employees faced a dilemma. They were paid excellent wages and had their full measure of hours off while at work they were driven so hard, each doing the work of three that they wondered if it was not a case of a reversed metaphor — what you gain on the swings you lose on the roundabouts . . .

Salesgirls and departmental managers apart, however, two men — or at least one of them — considered they had every reason to grumble.

One of the two was Clayton Ross, the head dispenser, and the other was Stuart Jones, his assistant. Between them, buried beneath the busy ground floor of the emporium, they were responsible for making up an endless stream of prescriptions and when the stream slowed a little, for the creation of sinister patent medicines which, though fully authorized, might have done better service down the drain.

Clayton Ross, whilst fully qualified for his responsible dispensary position, was as yet only thirty and had worked in the emporium since it had opened two years ago. He was one of the few who had seen the Boss frequently.

He was tall, thin, with untidy fair hair and exceptionally pale-grey eyes. He talked wildly, worked hard, and had a habit of nursing up grievances, and then in one deluge of words he would get them all off his chest and afterwards never refer to them again.

'The conditions some people have to work under are a disgrace!' Clayton Ross said, tilting a bottle of rosy fluid into a beaker and studying it critically. 'Politicians are always talking about improvements for the daily employee — but they never get to the root of the thing. There are still thousands of workers suffering as we are!'

Stuart Jones, Scotch on his mother's side and Welsh on his father's, had fallen between two stools and emerged as a characterless-looking, tow-headed young man of twenty-five, the key to his whole nature indicated in a chin which was merely a button of flesh under his lower lip. He was a good chemist because his father had forced him to be, but otherwise he was decidedly less than dynamic.

'Slavery!' Clayton Ross added broodingly. 'The conditions we work under, Stu, are a disgrace! Look at this basement — hardly enough room to turn round. For an emporium this size we ought to have something much bigger. We're always bumping into one another — which might be dangerous if we happened to be carrying acid — and we're imprisoned amongst all sorts of unhealthy fumes.'

'It is a bit badly arranged,' Jones agreed mildly.

'Badly arranged!' Ross hooted. 'Under here we have all the area of the ground sales floor — but what do we get personally? *This* mousetrap! Three parts of it are taken up in chemical stock and equipment, and we who do all the work sweat and toil with never a glimpse of daylight . . . '

'That doesn't matter much in this weather,' Jones observed philosophically.

'Of course everything conforms to law in regard to ventilation, lighting, standard of health, and so on . . . ' Ross admitted grudgingly. 'But unless the Boss makes some kind of alteration and gives us more room I'm thinking of going.'

'That's a far more likely possibility than us getting better quarters — and you know it,' Jones responded. 'I doubt the Boss will change things just to suit us. If you don't like it, somebody else will. That's his policy.'

Ross poured out some more rosy fluid. 'You know, the trouble is that this blasted emporium is squeezed on too small a plot of land. Pity is that the shops around can't be knocked down and make room for the emporium to spread, and our quarters with it. The Boss is always saying he wants to extend.'

'Why can't the shops be knocked

down?' Stuart Jones asked, quite logically.

'Can't be done. Red tape. I read all about it in a Council meeting report. You know how the Boss is always telling the Council to get an abrogation of the land laws for Halingford? You should read your paper, Stu, and keep in touch with what's going on in your own district . . . There are three points in this neighbourhood with shops on 'em which prevent anybody buying any land in that area. Something about them surviving in perpetuity or something. Anyway, it means that as long as they stand the rest of the area is untouchable — cannot be bought, altered, or anything. Otherwise the Boss would have bought up the entire town by now.'

'Which,' Jones sighed, finishing bottling some liniment, 'doesn't look any too good for us, does it?'

Ross put down the bottle of rosy fluid. 'I think I'll ask the Boss what he can do to improve our position. I'll tell the Boss just what it is we need to make things comfortable. I don't see how he can refuse. I'm not afraid of him!'

Since Jones had never said he was, he

met the challenging stare of the grey eyes with equanimity.

'Twenty past five,' Ross said, glancing at the clock. 'By half past he should be alone in his office — getting ready to clear out as usual at six. I'll pop up and see him. If he turns nasty I can always give my notice.'

'Or receive it,' Jones suggested helpfully.

Ross began unpacking a carton of toothbrushes. 'I'd risk anything to be the chief of a really large upstairs dispensary with daylight and plenty of assistants . . . In fact I've *got* to have it before I can reasonably ask Claire to marry me.'

'Is Claire that sort of a girl?' Jones asked artlessly.

'I don't know, but I can't ask her to leave her stage career for a pig-in-a-poke, and that's all it would be on my present screw. She hasn't actually said *what* she wants, but I've a pretty good idea. After her sort of life, knocking about all over the place, she'll naturally need something really nice when she does decide to settle down.'

'Stage career?' Jones repeated, puzzling. 'In the chorus?'

'She has hopes of becoming a musical comedy star,' Ross explained, defending Claire Denbury — third from the right on the front row of girls — to the limit. 'One day she'll get sick of touring round — she's in Birmingham this week — and when that day comes I need to offer her something good. That means I've got to improve on this.'

Silence. The flow of oral lava had stopped. He finished unpacking the toothbrushes, and then looked at the clock again. On the stroke of 5.30 he left the dispensary and took the lift to Rupert Granwell's sumptuous office on the top floor.

In five minutes Clayton Ross was back in the dispensary.

He did not speak, but to Stuart Jones' surprise there was a blank amazement in his pale-grey eyes and a tautness edging into fear about his lips. He looked as though he had either had a gigantic shock or else had an interview with Lucifer.

3

The grey February afternoon was already commencing to blur into frosty twilight, tinged with mist when Gordon Drew arrived in Sundale Avenue and looked again upon the residence where he had been born and reared.

It was the only one of its kind in this select residential quarter — inevitably Georgian, with the customary two round pillars at either side of the portico.

It stood squarely in its own large grounds, its defects hidden by the all-over yellowish varnish so common to such houses. In fact it looked as though this exterior polish had only been added recently.

As Gordon Drew remembered it upon departure the paint had been peeling off in strips, presenting a leprous and entirely decrepit appearance. There were other repairs he could detect too. Everything had apparently been brought up to date.

He smiled pensively as he leaned upon the low iron rail separating the perfectly kept gardens from the street. Standing here, weaving remembrances out of the past, Gordon lost track of time completely. He was merely conscious of the steadily lowering twilight and of the half-formed thought at the back of his mind that he must be on his way to the station — and London, and, he hoped, a job.

'What the devil do you mean by loitering on my railing like that? This is a private house and not a museum!'

Thus addressed in a high-pitched, impatient voice, Gordon straightened up and gazed towards the house. In the dying light he could see a figure standing in the front doorway under the portico. The figure was small and the voice a man's. He was standing with his hands thrust in his trousers pockets, gazing out into the evening.

Gordon remembered something Janice Lloyd had said about this individual being either downright rude, absentminded, or else plain crazy. At the moment the first qualification seemed to fit.

'A cat can look at a king, sir,' Gordon commented dryly.

'The metaphor is wrong,' the figure observed. 'We are discussing the fact that you are viewing my house. The house is obviously inorganic, therefore you cannot possibly draw an analogy between it and a king. Nor for that matter can you draw a parallel between yourself and a cat.'

This extraordinary outburst of logic, albeit slightly cockeyed, arrested Gordon's fancy completely. The man was worthy of a place in Alice in Wonderland. Gordon made up his mind on the moment, unfastened the familiar wrought-iron gate and strolled up the long front path.

The man came out to meet him and Gordon observed his extraordinary smallness — not more than four feet ten — and sprouting mane of grey hair which stood out Einstein-fashion all round his massive head.

'Dr. Carruthers?' Gordon asked at length.

'Any objections? Yes, I am Dr. Carruthers, and I do not inhabit a public exhibition but a private house. And I don't like loiterers. At this time of year it can't be the beauty of the garden you were admiring, so it must have been the house. I want to know why!'

It became clear to Gordon that this business called for tact. 'I humbly apologize for leaning on the rail and studying the house like that, Doctor — '

'So I should hope! I saw you from my study window. If you're planning on burgling the place some night I should think again. I'm a scientist, and I know how to take every precaution.'

'I was simply reviving old memories. Once I used to live in this very house. I'm Gordon Drew.'

'Drew? Drew?' The gnome mused in the gathering dark. Then in surprise, 'Of course! I seem to remember that Mrs. Dodd, the wife of the man who died just after buying this place from your father, mentioned your name . . . I never forget names. In fact I never forget *anything*. Well now, that's different. Taking a walk down memory lane, eh?'

'Yes,' Gordon admitted, 'you might call it that.'

‘In that case, come inside. You can’t revive memories by staring at the outside of a building. You need to come inside and look at the familiar nooks and corners. If you find dust don’t blame me. I’m incurably Bohemian.’

Suddenly he had disappeared inside the front doorway. Gordon followed. The light was not on but this was no deterrent to him: he knew the way by heart.

At the opposite end of the hall a yellow glow sprang into being from what, in his days of occupation here, had been the lounge. Now . . .

It seemed to be part office, study, and junk room, lighted by a single two-hundred watt lamp with a yellow shade round it. Carruthers had used the word ‘Bohemian’, which had been a complete understatement. ‘Bedlam’ might have been more appropriate.

The predominant article of furniture was a massive desk. Here and there the leather top was visible, but for the most part it was smothered in all manner of papers. There were a row of steel filing cabinets against the wall by the window;

then came a massive safe. In another corner were three bookcases of differing sizes and each one of them crammed with volumes thick and thin, horizontal and vertical. Then came the massive marble mantelshelf.

In the grate a fire was burning cheerily, casting a pleasant warmth along the well-carpeted floor towards the armchair, which judging from the dents in the cushions was accustomed to a good deal of use.

'Damned awful mess,' Dr. Carruthers said, holding forth a gold cigarette case. 'Still, if you ignore the room's contents you may be able to visualize it as once it was.'

'We used it as the lounge,' Gordon explained. 'Mother particularly liked the view through these windows on to the lawns.'

'Uh-huh — if you've time to look outside. I've precious little time for anything except my work. I don't particularly like windows: even less do I like working near them. They're draughty for one thing, and they distract your attention. That was why you annoyed me. Through the window I could see you leaning on the railing and I asked myself what in hell you could want.'

As Dr. Carruthers felt for the matchbox with which to light the cigarettes, Gordon took the opportunity to study him.

His features were remarkable. There was of course that massive head and brow, then came a curved nose and jutting lips and jaw. Force radiated from the man, as it did from the shrewd sky-blue eyes that gazed over the match-flame as he held it forward. The only thing lacking was height, but like so many people of indifferent stature Carruthers had all the assertiveness of a bantam.

'Naturally,' Gordon said, 'I appreciate your allowing me to see the old place like this, but I've no wish to be inquisitive. Your house is your own and — '

'You needn't fear that the rest of it is in the same appalling condition as this room,' Carruthers grinned, revealing very white artificial teeth. 'My housekeeper — to put it vulgarly — is a fusspot. Keeps the rest of the place like a showpiece: damned sight more interested in it than I am myself. Give some women a house or a business to fiddle with and they'll do things to it you'd never even dream of — sensible things sometimes too. Don't know what I'd do without Mrs. Barret. All the same, I've threatened her with instant death if she dares to touch a thing in here. This part of the house is sacrosanct. Where I know where everything is.'

Gordon Drew reflected that certainly nobody else ever would.

An imperious hand guided him to sit in the armchair by the fire. Gordon obeyed and Carruthers pulled up a smaller armchair and sat down opposite him, just like a little boy with the head and face of a Beethoven.

'You're probably thinking that it's unusual to invite a stranger into one's house after insulting him,' Carruthers said dryly.

'I can quite understand your first impressions. I must have looked like a loiterer.'

Carruthers scowled into the fire. 'I've a damned silly habit of shooting first and questioning afterwards. Doesn't do sometimes . . . Have some tea? It's not very hot. I make one pot to last me all the afternoon.'

Without waiting for an answer, Carruthers had hopped to his feet and dived a hand unerringly into the lake of papers. On the end of his hand appeared a teapot, with a knitted cosy about it, clinging like a shrunken vest round a portly stomach.

Carruthers went over to a cupboard and brought out a cup and saucer, filled it with tea, added milk and sugar, and then handed it over. Once more diving into the papers with his hand he hauled out a used cup and saucer and got busy with the teapot again.

'Tea,' he explained, as Gordon sipped at the tepid stuff, 'is the finest stimulant on God's earth, and you can't get intoxicated on it. The colder it is the less the tannin affects you. You'll find all sorts of weird arguments put forth by men who ought to know better about the lining of your stomach getting a fur if you drink too much tea. There's some horrible analogy about a steam boiler that periodically needs scraping. Damned rot, of course. For the brain-worker, tea — hot, tepid, or cold — is essential!'

Gordon drank half of the tepid stuff and then handed it back. Carruthers looked at what was left and gave a grin.

'I'd do better only my housekeeper's out shopping,' he explained. 'It's more than my life's worth to go in her domain and brew tea. She knows this pot should last me until we have dinner at seven.'

'We?'

'Yes. You and I, Mr. Drew.'

'But I've got to get to London this evening. Thanks for the invitation, but I can't possibly stay.'

'Don't be absurd,' Dr. Carruthers said calmly.

Gordon kept remembering what Janice Lloyd had said — that Carruthers was probably crazy. Hardly that, surely . . . 'Peculiar', maybe . . . intensely individual.

'Look, son, I go round with my eyes and ears open. So let me tell you that I can think of only one reason for your going to London — to look for work. Am I right?'

Gordon looked his astonishment. The Beethovian face broke into a grin.

'You're thinking that I'm either a sort of Sherlock Holmes with deductive powers, or else a telepathist. I'm neither, even though I do believe in the immense possibilities of the latter science. It's simply that I happen to read the newspapers with extreme thoroughness. In fact it's part of my work . . . Through that medium I know what other observant people should also know . . . that Mr. Gordon Drew, formerly managing director of Electrical Products Limited, recently lost his fortune and his business through the destruction by fire of his entire concern. Since the said Mr. Drew was referred to as the son of Arthur Drew, formerly of Halingford, it obviously means you. The details were given — *inter alia* — in the *Daily Tatler* for January 10.'

Gordon smiled. 'Yes, I am that Gordon Drew. You have an excellent memory.'

'I never forget anything. Then you *are* looking for work? Or have you something saved up and intend to stick your neck out again?'

'It's my neck,' Gordon pointed out.

'Yes but you're young, boy. Too young to be turned loose amongst the vultures, and London's thick with 'em.'

'Yes,' Gordon agreed, 'it is. And I haven't anything saved up and even if I had I wouldn't risk speculating with it again. But I'm prepared to take a chance on something that doesn't need money.'

Carruthers threw his cigarette away into the fire. 'I'm a lonely man, Mr. Drew. Hardly anybody ever comes to see me, or if they do it's in a strictly professional capacity. As well as being lonely I'm infernally busy — witness this room. I've been thinking that I ought to get a secretary or somebody — a man of course. No time for women with their dust-removing penchants. Then you arrive and gaze at my place. Sort of seems like a thing which had to be, doesn't it?'

'My abilities as a secretary are exactly nil,' Gordon shrugged. 'In fact I don't like any job which is confining. Besides, what makes you willing to want me, on trust as it were? I've said I'm Gordon Drew, yes, but I *might* be planning a robbery or something.'

'If you are, then God help you with the gadgets I have lying round,' Carruthers chuckled. 'My house is fully proofed against attack. I've a good reason for it, of course. Some of the things I have in my laboratory are far in advance of their time and plenty of thieves might like to get their hands on them. However, you *are* Gordon Drew. Your photograph was in the *Sunday Illustrated* for June 14 last year, and again in the *Weekly Observer* for July 6, also last year. Playboy Gordon Drew does this, playboy Gordon Drew does that. You're Drew all right, and had it not been twilight outside I'd have recognized you at once.'

'I'm not a pen-pusher, Doctor.'

'Pen-pusher be damned, boy! My secretary must be somebody who's prepared for the unusual and unexpected . . . be ready to go anywhere and do many a strange thing. The clerical part is the least important . . . You *are* looking for work?'

'Yes . . . ' Gordon admitted, and then repeated the details as he had given them to Janice.

'Splendid!' Carruthers declared, sitting back in his armchair. 'You're just the kind of young man I've been looking for. I'm a scientist, or more exactly, I'm a physicist. I have connection with other scientists engaged on the problems of atomic energy. But nowadays I've severed my connections with the atomic group, and spend my time on less exacting matters, freed of Governmental restrictions. I'm writing a book on atomic physics, for one thing; I'm conducting experiments into filterable viruses for another — my laboratory is in the basement — and at times there are Scotland Yard and various police departments to look after.'

Gordon frowned. 'Oh? What have the police got to do with it?'

'Sometimes I help them, in almost any capacity.' Carruthers gave a dry smile. 'The police call on experts to help them now and again — experts in some particular field, just as the divisional-surgeon is in his particular field of medicine. I combine quite a few functions. I'm a sort of general specialist, replacing the need of several different specialists who have one-track minds. One journalist with more wit than I gave him credit for called me the 'Admirable Crichton' of scientific specialists. I rather liked that . . . So you see,' Carruthers shrugged, 'my work isn't exactly dull, though as my secretary don't expect that you'll have thrill piled upon thrill and turn into a sort of Bulldog Drummond. You won't. But it *will* be interesting.'

'Yes, there's no doubt of that,' Gordon agreed. 'From time to time, then, I suppose the police consult you?'

'Certainly.' Carruthers gave a direct look. 'That wouldn't worry you, would it? There isn't something I don't know which makes you anxious to avoid the police?'

'Why, no.' Gordon's expression did not change by one fraction. 'I'm wondering, though — murder is murder, isn't it? It's either a gun, a garrotting cord, a knife or poison. Rarely do you hear of anything unique in the way of killing people. All poisons leave a trace to the toxicologists — despite what crime-writers say; death rays and things that kill at a distance don't exist in the practical sense. Where does a physicist come in?'

'The modern criminal, my boy, is highly scientific,' Carruthers answered. 'The modern crook is so damnably clever a solution is rarely found, and so the business is played down. That's where I come in — and other experts like me. We are dedicated to the task of defeating the criminal who makes use of modern methods to perpetrate his or her villainy. It's a branch of crime still in its infancy, but another army is growing up to strangle it. Why else do you imagine the Yard has become so highly scientific these days? Only to keep pace with the ever more subtle ways of the scientific evil-doer . . . ' Carruthers broke off and went to the teapot. 'That's made me dry,' he said.

He drank a half-cupful of the muck and then gave Gordon a questioning glance.

'I need a chap like you — young, obviously intelligent, who's had the hard corners knocked off. You need work, so we can help each other very nicely. There's another reason. There isn't much of me, as you'll have noticed — a fact which I don't regret, mind you, because I believe that a great brain usually goes with a small body — but I need a man with youth and strong muscles to — er — do his stuff sometimes. So . . . Everything will be found and you'll have plenty of liberty. As for money — well, we won't quarrel over that, I'm sure.'

Gordon heard every word even though he was thinking of Janice Lloyd. It had been hard work wrenching himself away from her. Had he possessed some sort of security he never would have done it. And some sort of security he might even yet achieve if he helped this eccentric ex-atom scientist.

'It's a deal, Doctor,' he said abruptly, rising to his feet. 'I'll take it on.'

4

When it came to knowing how to get the ultimate value out of a steak of cod or fillet of sole there was no man in Halingford the equal of Mr. Oscar Bilkin, the fishmonger and fruiterer in the High Street.

The high-ups and lowly folk alike bought from him. He had two neat little vans that carried his goods in stiff proof paper to the customers on most days of the week.

In twenty years of honest dealing he had built up a prosperous business — at the cost, unfortunately, of acquiring a permanent effluvium reminiscent of low tide under a jetty. He was a friend of everybody, including the police, and many had been the times when children were his customers that he had added two extra plums to the pound for their especial benefit.

Oddly enough, Oscar Bilkin did not

look the soul of good cheer. He was small and spare, with extremely narrow shoulders, a very thin face, and large disproportionate hands that seemed to be all knuckles.

The purplish tint at the end of his nose was definitely the outcome of indigestion and not, as his few competitors swore, the result of too-frequent visits to the Swan and Duckling. In winter or summer he wore a cap so flat it appeared to have been under a hydraulic press. Invariably he sported hobnailed boots and stiff leather leggings, which latter gave his scrawny calves an apparent development entirely superficial.

Thus attired, in a faded blue suit, he served fish and vegetables from nine until five in the afternoon, at which hour — or earlier if he had sold out — he closed to the public and indulged in a solid hour of cleaning, scrubbing, brushing, and preparation, making the fish slabs so spotless that at a pinch a surgeon could have placed a patient on any of them and performed a major operation.

At the back of this façade of fish, fruit

and vegetables and the everlasting odorous admixture of fish, earth, and onions, there moved his wife — a monstrous woman whose generosity was a byword and whose scale measurements when she occasionally looked after the shop were mere guesswork to the benefit of the customer . . .

And his daughter Edith, a young lady of modern ideas happily allied to a full consciousness of her responsibility. She, in slacks and woollen jumper, drove one of the vans religiously every day and spent her off-moments with a similar van-driving spouse who collected and delivered for the Spotless Wash Limited.

The Bilkin's second van was usually driven by a youth of nineteen, whose attention was completely centred on the results of Halingford football team. Young Bert, in fact, had no other interest in life outside soccer. Even girls couldn't distract him from it.

Altogether, then, the Bilkin family was a happy one — making money in a quiet, honest way and perfectly contented with its lot. Thus it was all the more extraordinary to find that such a man as Oscar Bilkin, liked throughout the community, should be singled out to receive the message . . . It came by the post on the day after Gordon Drew had peregrinated into town.

The message was in an ordinary cheap buff envelope and, the shop being just closed for lunch, the postman had pushed it through the letterbox. It had fallen face down on the shop floor and when he came to re-open the shop for the afternoon customers Mr. Bilkin found the missive lying there.

He picked it up and glanced — then stared. The extraordinary method of address made him start. Words — no, letters — had apparently been cut painstakingly from a newspaper and glued to the envelope to form his name in shaky lines:

MR. O. BILKIN,
17, HALINGFORD ROAD,
HALINGFORD.
LOCAL.

'Well, I'm perished!' observed Mr. Bilkin, and returned into the kitchen with his prize. He went across to where his wife and daughter were clearing the dinner things and showed them the envelope in a kind of puzzled wonder. His wife looked at it in surprise.

'Why, Ozzy, what is it? Who on earth would want to send you an envelope addressed in that funny way?'

Edith looked and said, 'Huh, that's queer!' Then she waited, wide-eyed, for something to happen as her father opened the envelope.

Then Mr. Bilkin received his second shock. More words cut from a newspaper and glued on to a single sheet of notepaper:

GET OUT BEFORE TOMORROW. YOU ARE ALL IN DANGER.

'Well, I'm perished!' Mr. Bilkin exclaimed finally, seeming to find his vocabulary limited to this observation.

'Now I *know* it's some sort of joke,' his wife observed, smiling.

'But — but Ma, who'd want to play a joke like this? It isn't as though it's the first of April. It's the tenth of February.'

'Well, of *course* it's a joke, Dad!'

daughter Edith corroborated. 'What else can it be? Probably Charlie Wagshaw.'

Charlie Wagshaw was the local dentist, and perhaps because his profession was so unfunny he had a disturbing habit in his spare time of perpetrating practical jokes on all and sundry. There were few of his acquaintances in Halingford who had not had their handshakes enlivened with a palm-buzzer, or found a jet of icy water streaming in their faces from an innocent 'rose' on his coat lapel.

But that Wagshaw should send a message like this was — to Oscar Bilkin anyway — like suggesting that the Mayor had publicly announced his intention of playing marbles.

'No, I don't think Charlie's at the back of this.' Mr. Bilkin's flat cap moved from side to side as he shook his head. 'I believe,' he finished with a touch of awe, 'it might even be a *real* warning!'

'Aw go on with you!' With that, his wife turned to the more practical duty of clearing of the crockery.

Edith considered her father in concern as she noticed the worry on his thin face

— then conscious of her limitations, she turned back to helping her mother.

'I think I'd better go and ask Charlie if he's back of it,' Mr. Bilkm said at last. 'Have an eye to the shop, Mother.'

'All right but . . . Just a minute, Father! You're not going to step out and make a fool of yourself, are you? That note's obviously a joke, and if Charlie Wagshaw did write it he'll laugh himself silly when he sees how worried it's made you . . . I don't much like the idea of you going out to be laughed at.'

'I don't like the idea from start to finish,' Mr. Bilkin said. 'There's been a good deal of trouble attached to sending this note. Every letter has been cut out separately. Why should anybody go to all that trouble just for a *joke*? It doesn't make sense.'

Just for a moment a cloudy suspicion of real danger crossed Mrs. Bilkin's mind — then evaporated almost immediately. Get out, indeed! Where to, anyway? And with a prosperous business to be taken care of. 'I think,' she said, 'the best thing you can do is throw it in the fire.'

‘But supposing something did happen? It would be evidence, wouldn’t it?’

‘Evidence?’ repeated Mrs. Bilkin vaguely, who did not read thrillers.

‘I’m bothered even if you are not,’ Mr. Bilkin added. ‘I’ll go and see Charlie and one or two of the other boys. If I think they didn’t do it I’ll go to the police.’

Mrs. Bilkin nodded her grey head. After all, there *might* be something in it, and if so the law was a necessity and a comfort. Edith’s thoughts on the business did not signify. To her parents still a child despite her appearance of adult maturity.

So, with the strange letter and envelope in his pocket, Mr. Bilkin went along to the dentist’s fifty yards down the street. No — Charlie Wagshaw had not sent it. In fact he was hurt at the thought of his practical joking technique being held in such low esteem.

Mr. Bilkin also had this reassurance from three other friends who had leanings towards the unexpected. So, with nebulous thoughts about poison pens and sinister blackmailers, Mr. Bilkin finished his brief tour of inquiry in the police station.

There was only one official present to commence with — Sergeant Mead who, being unwilling to take the responsibility unto himself, brought on the scene Detective-Sergeant Grant. He knew the fishmonger well.

'Well, Ozzy — hello! Anything wrong?'

Detective-Sergeant Grant was about thirty-two and only took the liberty of calling Mr. Bilkin 'Ozzy' because everybody else did so. Grant was considered to be a smart man — tall, round-faced, blond-headed, of superb physique, and he certainly was not lacking in acumen either. He came across to the inquiry counter.

'I'm worried, Bob,' Mr. Bilkin explained, tugging the note out of its envelope and laying it down. 'See what you can make of this. It came around noon in the post today.'

Grant read the note through with a puzzled frown and then studied the envelope. 'Posted in Halingford . . . And you have no idea as to who might have sent it?'

'Not the remotest. I've just spent the best part of an hour asking some of my friends — the practical joker kind — if they had anything to do with it. But they say none of them did this. I'm satisfied they weren't lying, either, so what I'm wondering is: does it mean something? Is it a real warning?'

Grant rubbed the back of his red neck. 'You haven't any enemies, Ozzy, have you? Who'd want to bring harm to you, or Mrs. Bilkin and Edith?'

'As far as I know,' the fishmonger answered quietly, 'I'm a friend of everyone in this town — bar none. But suppose some crazy person, or a poison-pen writer — the kind you read about in the Sunday papers — is at the back of this?'

'I shouldn't pay too much attention to what you read in the Sunday papers, Ozzy; and as for this note I think you'd better see the Super. Come on.'

The detective-sergeant raised the counter-flap and Mr. Bilkin accompanied him across the main enquiry room to a private office. Superintendent Clifford Denning was within, reading through some closely typed notes.

‘If you have a moment, sir,’ Grant apologized, as he entered. ‘Rather a puzzling business has come up. You know Mr. Bilkin?’

‘Yes, indeed.’ Superintendent Denning got up from his desk and shook hands.

Denning had dark hair and eyes with a geniality that disguised the inner keenness of his nature. Those in the know were satisfied that sheer ability was the sole reason for him being in charge of the Halingford police. Certainly the Chief Constable of the county, Colonel Barrow, had no fault to find with this thirty-eight-year-old policeman.

Mr. Bilkin sat down and waited as Grant did all the talking and explaining. He watched as the superintendent returned to his chair and studied the note carefully.

‘And this dropped out of a clear sky?’ he asked at last.

‘That’s right, Super,’ Mr. Bilkin agreed. ‘I’ve been to see several of my pals to see if they’d sent it, but they haven’t. I’m worried. If it isn’t a joke what does it mean? There’s no possible reason for wanting to hurt me or perhaps damage my property. I'd like to think it's some kind of a hoax — only if it isn't where would I be then? Or my missus and kid?'

'Yes, indeed. Is your property insured, Mr. Bilkin?'

'Of course! Been insured nearly fifteen years with the Paragon Company. I took good care of that. If anything happens to that place I collect. Does it matter?'

'I only wondered in case anything *should* happen.' Denning said. 'At the moment, Mr. Bilkin, there is nothing we can do except see what happens. Probably this thing is a cruel, misguided hoax. If that be so we cannot of course waste our time trying to trace the perpetrator. We'll only get busy if something startling really does happen.'

'And leave me to stand waiting for it?' Mr. Bilkin asked in alarm.

'Not quite.' Denning smiled reassuringly. 'You are fully entitled to police protection if you want it. What I will do is have Saunders — he's a good man — come along this afternoon and look your place over. That is, if you wish it?'

'Most certainly I do.'

'Good. I have no authority to have a man examine your property unless you ask for it. I'll have Saunders look for anything suspicious. If he finds anything he will report to me and you will naturally get out. In any case he will keep a watch on your property until after tomorrow, by which time whatever is going to happen will have — unless of course we can prevent it. Saunders will be relieved by Marsden, an equally alert chap.'

'That makes me feel a lot happier,' Mr. Bilkin said, with his first smile.

'Just doing our job, Mr. Bilkin. Immediately Saunders reports for duty — around three o'clock — I'll send him over.'

'And the note? Do I keep it?'

'We'll keep that, sir. Never know but what we might need it.'

Quite satisfied, Oscar Bilkin departed for home. He gave his wife the details. In the interval of his absence she had had time to think, and that had fostered a gathering anxiety. Now it was considerably dispelled.

It was banished completely when at

quarter past three P. C. Saunders arrived.

He was tall, broad-shouldered, and deferential. Without apparently disturbing anything or anybody he went over the premises from top to bottom, utilizing all his constable's training to look for suspicious objects, even in the most extraordinary places.

He even borrowed a pair of overalls from Mr. Bilkin and spent some time full length under the floors of the place, flashing his torch beam into every angle and corner.

He ended his search two hours later, convinced there was nothing suspicious on the Bilkin property. This fact he reported promptly to the superintendent.

'Probably a hoax after all, then,' Denning said, 'but we'd better be sure. Stay on the watch, Saunders. Marsden will relieve you later.'

'Right, sir.'

During the remainder of the day nothing untoward happened though Mr. and Mrs. Bilkin remained alert, Edith being in the van making the afternoon deliveries.

Anyone other than regular customers of the shop was subjected to intense scrutiny. It never occurred to either Mr. or Mrs. Bilkin that a would-be attacker would hardly carry his or her weapon in a shopping basket. And anyway the note had said tomorrow.

The night passed uneventfully.

Mr. and Mrs. Bilkin slept soundly and Edith spent eight happy hours dreaming fitfully of her Lothario aboard his laundry van — then at six o'clock the dream world was gone into icy February dawn and activity spread itself over mother, father, and daughter.

Each had a particular job — mother to prepare the breakfast, Edith to warm up the engines on the vans — incredibly recalcitrant in the frost — and father to stack up the vegetables and await the eight o'clock arrival of the ice-man.

Though it savoured of carrying coals to Newcastle in such weather, the ice-man came daily from the Cold Ice Company bringing one massive block which Mr. Bilkin always smashed up and afterwards laid his choicest fish cuts upon its shattered remains.

Mr. Bilkin was arranging cabbages when a heavy pounding on the closed front door made him start. He went across and opened it to behold a policeman in the mist and frost outside. Since it was not Saunders it was presumably Marsden. He saluted respectfully.

''Morning, sir. Everything all right?'

'Perfectly,' Mr. Bilkin assented, blowing on his hands. 'Nothing happened during the night?'

'No, sir. Nothing . . . '

Bilkin drew the door wider. 'Come inside, Constable, and have a cup of tea.'

'Thank you, sir. It is a bit chilly.'

Bilkin motioned through to the kitchen, knowing his wife would do the rest, then he returned to his deployment of the vegetables. Edith came into the shop after a moment or two, blowing on the ends of her fingers.

'I hate starting up vans in this weather Dad,' she remarked, but here her tendency to grumbling stopped and she turned willingly to help him with the shop arrangements.

One of her jobs was the writing on the

small blackboard giving the price of the day's fish supply — which at this moment her father was slicing up with knife and mallet.

It took both of them twenty minutes, after which time Edith had her particular vegetables sorted out for the vans and P.C. Marsden was emerging from the kitchen, drawing on his white knitted gloves.

'Much obliged, sir. I'll be going off duty shortly and Saunders will take over.'

He went outside and departed along the pavement to his vantage point. He had hardly done so before the familiar wagon of the Cold Ice Company drew up very gently outside, steam pouring from its dirty radiator.

'Here's Bill, Dad,' Edith said. 'Early, too! I'll open the window for you.'

She hurried outside and seized hold of the brass clamps at the base of the big window's lower sash. Straining to the limit she raised the frame until it was flush behind the upper sash and the spotless imitation marble slab ready for the ice-block.

Edith dug her numbed hands in her

slacks pockets and waited, watching the van. It surprised her to notice that the ice blocks were covered up this morning. Usually they were there for anyone to see, but today a huge, stiff tarpaulin had been thrown over them.

'What's the idea, Bill?' she called. 'Afraid of your ice blocks catching cold?'

To her surprise it was not the familiar Bill Higgins who jumped down from the truck but a burly stranger in a reefer coat and greasy cap.

He glanced towards her, nodded, then went round to the particular ice block consigned to Mr. Bilkin and drew it from under the tarpaulin. It was wrapped in thick felt, leaving the ends open, and with infinite care the man worked it on to his shoulder.

'Don't hurt it!' Edith called to him dryly. 'Why don't you put your tongs round it?'

'What's the odds so long as you get it?' he demanded, and came across the pavement with it.

Very carefully, as though it were a newly born baby, he laid it on the marble slab and carefully drew the felt from around it.

'Looks a bit dirty,' Edith commented, frowning. 'More yellow than usual. What's it made from — river water?'

'All I do is deliver the stuff and I'm new to the job,' the man said. 'I'll sling the stuff about fast enough when I get used to it. Give me a chance, can't you?'

'What happened to Bill Higgins?' Mr. Bilkin asked, as he signed the invoice.

'Dunno. On another round, I think. The boss put me on this one, so there it is.'

'You're confoundedly early, anyway,' Edith remarked. 'And what's the idea of driving the truck as though you're going to a funeral?'

'Cold engine, of course. What else d'you expect in this perishin' weather?' The man grimaced, and took the invoice. 'Thanks, Mr. Bilkin. Good mornin'.'

Without wasting any time he hurried across the pavement and jumped into the truck, set it going again with a grinding roar and rumbled off down the street.

'It does look a bit dirty,' Mr. Bilkin

admitted, studying the block. 'Maybe some sort of preserving chemical they're putting in it.'

Edith glanced at it again. It was a big block — three feet long by two wide by half a foot thick, the size her father usually had. When broken up it just made a comfortable layer for the slabs.

'He's a careful one, he is,' Edith said. 'Handling ice just as though it were table jelly or something. Did you see all that felt he had it wrapped up in? If he sticks on the job long he'll not be anything like so choosy.'

'You'd better get your orders to the vans, love,' her father said finally. 'I'll get this broken up and then we'll have breakfast.'

He turned aside to his hammer and chisel as Edith whisked up the first delivery basket and vanished through the kitchen en route to the backyard.

She had just put the basket in the van, was half in and half out of the vehicle, when the thing happened —

She was suddenly hurled bodily across the yard and struck her head with such resounding impact she was instantly knocked senseless.

In the kitchen Mrs. Bilkin stumbled under an avalanche of bricks and plaster as the room fell in on her. By some fluke she was hurled under the solid deal kitchen table, and the top took the weight of the rubble and left her still conscious but completely buried. Immediately she began the struggle to free herself, blood running down her right arm.

Further up the street P.C. Marsden was blown off his feet but remained conscious.

He, and many others in the street at the time, were treated to a terrific explosion — and simultaneously the fish and vegetable establishment of Mr. Bilkin belched outwards in an avalanche of bricks, wood, mortar, plaster, and smoke.

It made a report that was heard from one end of Halingford to the other and it left behind a huge smoking crater with the half-shattered ruins of the two adjoining premises looming drunkenly over the space where it had been.

5

Seated at breakfast in the spacious morning room of Dr. Carruthers' home, Gordon Drew had a feeling of unreality. There seemed to be something utterly incongruous about the furniture and the small, incisive little man with the shock of grey hair who had become his employer.

Today Gordon was prepared to start work in earnest — filing most of the little scientist's notes in connection with his book on atomic physics. It would not be exciting but at least it would pass the time until something really interesting came along.

Yesterday had been spent in assimilating what Carruthers had called 'the sense of things', and trying to remember all manner of details — the exact position of everything in the crazy den where the scientist worked, the reason for this sheet of computations, the reason for that filing cabinet, and so forth. This, together with an assessment of the laboratory in the basement, remarkably tidy for such an otherwise untidy man, had caused Gordon to fill a notebook with signposts for his own guidance in the wilderness.

The more he was in his new employer's company the more he found himself liking him. Though fiercely intolerant on the surface there was a sterling worth in the man. One moment he would be heartily upbraiding all and sundry — from politicians to housekeepers — for their damned incompetence, and the next he would be excusing them on the grounds that being anything but a perfect man himself he had no right to criticize. Conceit and modesty were forever trying to get the mastery of him.

Terms for salary had proved to be generous, and that he was a man of stupendous energy Gordon had guessed from the start. This fact was verified when he found breakfast was served punctually at seven so that the day's work could begin at eight.

It was ten past seven at the moment and Gordon found himself — at his employer's behest — with half a morning newspaper, while Carruthers read the other half. There were two metal stands on the table, complete with clips, intended for this very purpose.

'Use the moments, my boy,' Carruthers had said on the previous morning, when first explaining this procedure. 'And don't just *skim* through your paper — *read* it! And pay particular attention to crime and the latest scientific developments because that's where our interests lie.'

Which was exactly what Gordon Drew was doing now, while at the same time he tackled a most appetizing breakfast.

Opposite him, Carruthers had almost entirely vanished behind his own section of paper. 'I wouldn't be surprised if one of these days some bright spark makes use of the by-products of atomic fission,' his voice commented presently. 'The possibilities, you know, are endless. Did you ever — '

Then it happened — and they both felt it.

The shock of a tremendous explosion that made the windows rattle from air concussion while simultaneously there was a transient swaying of the floor.

'What the devil was that?' Carruthers demanded. 'Sounded like an atomic bomb!'

They waited for a possible repetition. None came. Finally the little scientist glanced at his watch. 'Seven twenty-five. Always worth noting the time of a strange happening.'

As they cautiously resumed their breakfast, there came more unexpected sounds. First, the clanging of a fire engine's bell, then the busier little bell of an ambulance. All this suggestion of activity operating just out of sight was obviously proving too much for Dr. Carruthers for he finally abandoned breakfast and jumped to his feet.

'Come on, Gordon!' he ordered. 'Must be something big going on and I'm not the type to sit still and miss it. Get yourself ready — we're going out!'

A few minutes later both men were leaving the house together and Gordon was treated to the surprising sight of the physicist in outdoor regalia.

He wore an overcoat that was abnormally long, having a belt twisted round the middle. A black homberg was perched on the back of his mane of grey hair; it seemed more of a token gesture to convention than actually useful.

They turned the corner of the avenue and entered the main road into Halingford proper. The view half a mile further down the road was self-explanatory. The area was thick with people; black smoke was rolling into the dreary February sky; there was a wilderness of hose-piping trailing about the street.

'This,' Carruthers remarked, glancing up at Gordon beside him, 'looks interesting!' They gained the stricken area in perhaps seven minutes. Pausing at the rear of the inquisitive throng they stood looking at the monstrous, smoking, gaping emptiness where Mr. Bilkin's fish and vegetable shop had been.

Being short in stature, Carruthers did not get a good enough view to suit him, and so began to elbow his way amongst the men and women in front of him, until — with Gordon beside him — he came to the forefront of the spectators and found one of several policemen barring his path.

'Sorry, sir, no further,' the constable ordered. Then he looked down again at the little man. 'Oh, it's you, Dr. Carruthers! Sorry, sir — you can come through.'

Carruthers nodded, jerking his head, and Gordon followed him.

'Not you, sir,' the constable said. 'I can't let anybody through unless they have an official standing.'

'He's with me, officer,' Carruthers snapped. 'My secretary. And you'd better get used to seeing him around.'

The constable saluted and stood to one side.

Carruthers ambled close to the scene where the firemen were busily working and Superintendent Denning stood comparing notes with Detective-Sergeant Grant.

'What goes on, Super?' Carruthers asked him interestedly, and Denning turned in surprise.

'Oh, hello, Doctor.' He knew Carruthers well, chiefly because Carruthers made it his business to be known to all the police departments in the particular district — and there had been many of them — in which he happened to reside. 'You heard the explosion, I suppose?'

'I should think it must have been heard in Glasgow,' the scientist replied. 'And from the look of this empty space it must have been a good one. Used to be Bilkin's, didn't it? Damned good fish he sold too.'

'Yes,' Denning agreed. 'It used to be . . .' He stopped, considering Gordon interestedly, his eyes travelling automatically to the burn scar.

'Mr. Drew — my secretary assistant,' Carruthers introduced. 'Gordon, this is Superintendent Denning of the Halingford police, and Detective-Sergeant Grant.'

The three men exchanged nods. Then Carruthers considered the smoking ruin again.

'Whoever did this certainly did it properly. The adjoining properties look as though they'll fall down at any moment. Anybody hurt?'

'Bilkin himself died almost immediately,'

Denning answered. 'His wife and daughter were slightly injured and are now in hospital.'

Denning did not add to this information. He was perfectly sure of his own ability to handle the material side of the tragedy and being a good policeman he did not intend to share his knowledge with any person unconnected with the police — not even with a man of Carruthers' reputation.

'I gather,' Carruthers said, with a glance about him, 'that you were sort of expecting this to happen?'

Denning frowned. 'How could I be?'

The grey mane jerked backwards. 'All these bobbies. Some of them are imported, presumably from Werton. You haven't got that many on your own force, and you couldn't have roped 'em in inside a few minutes. So you must have had an idea what was coming.'

'Even if I did, sir, it still represents official business,' Denning said, trying to be polite. 'I *did* have an inkling that something was going to happen and so took precautions . . . but I'd rather not say any more than that.'

Carruthers gave his gnome-like grin. 'I'm not trying to poke and pry; I've enough work of my own to do. But when a blast sufficient to knock me from the breakfast table disturbed my peace of mind I thought I'd look for the cause. Now I'm satisfied. Best of luck, Super.'

'Yes, sir — thank you.'

Carruthers turned back into the crowd. Before he and Gordon had got very far through it Gordon paused suddenly and gave a delighted exclamation.

'Jan! Of all people!' He dived from Carruthers' side and caught hold of Janice Lloyd's hand warmly as she stood in the crowd surveying the ruins.

'Hello, Gordon!' Happy surprise at discovering him still in the area was evident from her expression. 'I — I thought you'd gone to London?'

'I did intend. Instead I got myself a job here, with — '

'Me,' Carruthers interjected, and gave the girl a swift all-inclusive glance. 'Good morning, Miss Lloyd. Then you know our wandering boy?'

'And you know me?'

Carruthers looked disdainful. 'You've had your photo in the local paper often enough, haven't you? Glad to know you personally, Miss Lloyd.'

He shook her hand warmly and the three of them edged their way out of the busy throng to the outskirts. Then Janice seemed to think it necessary to explain herself.

'I heard the explosion and came out to see what had caused it. A perfectly dreadful business, isn't it? What in the world happened, I wonder?'

'Perhaps a leaking gas-pipe,' Carruthers said, shrugging. 'A tragedy. He sold such lovely fish . . . Well, Gordon, there's work to be done — if you're ready?'

Gordon hesitated, looking earnestly at Janice. 'Er — Jan, I — '

Carruthers said dryly, 'I think, Gordon, I had better excuse you for ten minutes while you unburden yourself to the young lady. I'm going on home — but join me there in ten minutes. No longer!'

'I definitely will, sir,' Gordon promised, with a grateful smile.

Carruthers went off up the road, a queer vest-pocket figure, hat on the back of his head, coat tails swinging. Janice looked after him and smiled faintly.

'What a funny little man he is, Gord!'

'And clever as they make 'em! I've found out the most amazing things about him in the brief time I've been staying with him. He isn't crazy — or anything approaching it. His chief interests at the moment are atomic physics and filterable viruses. Not that I know anything about either subject, but he seems to think that I can help him . . . ' Gordon broke off, gripping her arm.

'I was going to try and find time to call and see you and explain how things had turned out, but this chance has saved me the trouble. We must get together and renew the old friendship. There's no reason now why we shouldn't.'

Meanwhile, Denning was considering matters much less romantic. Grant and he were walking slowly round the edge of the now effectually obliterated fire, each holding a long stick, turning over the sodden, steaming ashes, dragging out of the way metallic articles which had survived the flames but lost their paint.

The watching crowd grew restive, and finally, as the firemen rolled up their hoses, began to disperse. Photographers came from the *Halingford Gazette* and focused their cameras on the scene, and after a while one of the reporters pursued the superintendent as he continued his laborious search for clues to explain the disaster.

'Any information for us, Super?' the reporter called from a little distance.

'Nothing yet, Meadows. If I have anything later I'll let you know.'

'We'll be reporting the fire, anyway. Suppose you've no idea what caused it?'

'No — so far. And I don't expect to have until these ashes have cooled off.'

The *Gazette* reporter hurried away. Denning came to a stop and sighed, moodily watching him depart. 'Haven't any information for ourselves, Grant, let alone him.'

'Queer business, sir,' Grant said, considering the blackened waste. 'And I don't think Saunders is the kind of man to have missed anything.'

'Neither do I. We'll have a word with him at his house. And when Marsden gets back from the hospital from having his hand treated we'll get his version too . . . ' Denning paused and watched a stranger picking his way through the blackened rubbish.

The newcomer was apparently a businessman, neatly attired in a blue Melton overcoat and wearing a bowler hat. As he came nearer he was revealed as about forty-five, his shrewd lantern-jawed face half concealed by a pair of horn-rimmed spectacles. He picked his way with the daintiness of a ballet dancer amidst the pools of water and debris, finally coming to a halt and batting irritably at his grey-striped trousers.

'You'll be — er — Inspector . . . ?' He gave a questioning look.

'Superintendent Denning,' Denning answered briefly. 'Of the Halingford police. Something I can do for you?'

'No — nothing. Only I like to make myself and my business clear to the authorities. I'm Amos Ballam, fire assessor. I'm acting on behalf of Mrs. Bilkin.'

Denning looked vague. 'You mean you're from the insurance company?'

'Not at all. They have their own experts. My duty is to secure for my client — in this instance, Mrs. Bilkin — the maximum possible compensation from her insurance company. My own fee is purely a percentage of the amount realized. In a word, Superintendent, I am an agent.'

'I see.' Denning nodded. 'Mrs. Bilkin know about this?'

'Of course. She asked the hospital to ring me up and come over at once to inspect the damage — so here I am. I'm from Werton,' he added, naming the large town five miles from Halingford. 'Here is my card. Mrs. Bilkin — or rather, Mr. Bilkin — had my name ready in case of any such happening as this at any time.'

The fire assessor sucked his teeth and surveyed the ruins. 'A truly nasty business, Superintendent. I believe poor Mr. Bilkin lost his life?'

'Yes. Died almost immediately.' Denning began to move. 'Anyway, Mr.

Ballam, make your assessment and afterwards give me a call at the police station, will you? I'd like a few words with you.'

'With pleasure,' the fire assessor agreed, and with that the superintendent and detective-sergeant left him to his explorations.

To the police still keeping back the throng Denning gave orders that three of them were to remain on duty for the time being in case anybody might remove valuable evidence under the pretext of getting a souvenir.

Then, after calling at P.C. Saunders' home for a few words, Denning and Grant returned to the police station and back into Denning's private office.

Moodily the superintendent sat down, pulled off his uniform cap, and motioned to a chair. Opening his desk drawer, Denning pulled out the original warning notice that Oscar Bilkin had received.

'It's damnable,' he muttered, tossing it on the desk. 'I'm left with the most disturbing feeling that I should have insisted on Bilkin, his wife, and daughter leaving those premises until after today.

My own inner belief that the whole thing was a joke has cost that poor devil his life.'

'You can't blame yourself, sir,' Grant remarked. 'You did all you could within the limits of the law. In any case, had you suggested him going, Bilkin would probably have refused for business reasons. And you had no power to make him.'

'That,' Denning said, 'does not alter my state of mind. I'll find out who did this diabolical thing, Grant, if it takes me the rest of my life! The note proves it must have been a premeditated act. There's one thing about it, though, which puzzles me. Why was it necessary to warn Bilkin to get out if the sole object was to blow him and his family sky high? Unless,' Denning added, thinking, 'the idea was to blow up the shop and give the family a chance to get clear.'

'Tracing the origin of the note isn't going to be easy,' Grant commented. 'Things sent through the mail are never an easy problem, and the old trick of cutting letters out of a newspaper is still pretty effective when it comes to confusing the trail.'

'Just the same, Grant, you're taking it over to the Werton police laboratories this very morning and have them see what the boys there can get out of it. I want every scrap of information they can find with their experts and facilities.'

Denning slipped note and envelope in a cellophane wrapper and handed it across. Grant nodded and put it away in his wallet. Using the Werton forensic laboratories was the accepted rule by the less well-equipped constabulary of Halingford.

'No gas accident or similar mishap could explain somebody knowing beforehand that it would happen,' Denning resumed. 'But if it were gas or something similar why didn't the Bilkins smell it beforehand? It must have been present in considerable quantity to cause an explosion of such terrific violence. I'm sure it was deliberate, and we have to find out how the devil it was done, and by whom. I might get some more light on it by having a chat with Mrs. Bilkin or her daughter. I'll slip over to the hospital while you go to Werton, but I'll have to stay for a while to see that fire assessor when he's finished. I want his professional opinion.'

'I suppose,' Grant said, rather doubtfully, 'he'll give it? If he happens to discover the fire — or explosion — was deliberately caused?'

Denning frowned, but he was interested. By experience he had come to know that there was a good deal of analytical reasoning went on in the detective-sergeant's mind. He had a faculty for looking a long way beyond surface appearance.

'We've no longer any reason to doubt it was a deliberate act, sir,' Grant said. 'And if that fact is discovered our friend Ballam will keep quiet, otherwise no insurance company in the land would tip up a penny. In fact they might even prosecute, and of course Ballam would not get his fee. All he will tell us is the part he wants us to know, unless he is a man of astounding honesty and reveals whatever trick it was that caused the explosion. The one we want to see is the insurance company's own assessor. He'll be coming when the claim's put through, to check up on behalf of the company and verify Ballam's findings.'

'That's true,' Denning admitted, surprised at how much his subordinate seemed to know concerning the workings of insurance. 'Anyway, I'll see Ballam . . . Yes, come in,' he invited, as there was a knock on the door.

It was P.C. Marsden who entered, his right arm in a sling and a look of supreme disgust on his beefy red face. He saluted somewhat clumsily with his sound hand.

'Glad you're back, Marsden,' the superintendent said, with a sympathetic smile. 'How bad's the hand?'

'Oh, nothing serious, sir. Be about ten days in a sling, or so the hospital tells me.'

'Sit down and tell me exactly what happened.'

Marsden took off his helmet and settled at the other side of the desk. 'To be candid, sir, I'm not at all sure. I'd just left Mr. Bilkin's shop and was going along Halingford Road — on the same side as the shop — and had taken up position in that little entry at the corner by the ironmonger's. It's a good spot to keep the Bilkin place under observation. I'd only been there about three minutes when the Bilkin shop exploded. I was knocked flying and damaged my hand. Some passers-by were also thrown over. Fortunately at that early hour there weren't many people about. It was twenty-five past seven.'

'I see. Then?'

'Immediately I'd picked myself up I rushed over to help, and so did the few passers-by. We managed to get out Mrs. Bilkin with a bad cut on her arm, and young Miss Bilkin from the yard. She'd been knocked senseless and had a gash over one eyebrow. We had a tough job on because there was a lot of smoke and fire and I was hampered by my injured hand. I told somebody to ring for the fire brigade and ambulance right away — which of course was done. We got Mr. Bilkin out from under the rubble at the front of the place . . . He was in a terrible state — I hardly like to think of it. He just lay looking at us — what there was left of him — and then he died.'

'And nobody called at the shop?' Denning questioned.

'Only the man delivering the day's ice. I saw him arrive and depart — but there was nobody else. In any case the shop wasn't open for customers that early. When I left after Mr. Bilkin told me all was well, he and his daughter were arranging the day's goods.'

'And only the ice-man called, eh?' Denning mused. 'Sure he was okay?'

'Far as I know he was, sir — yes. He had the Cold Ice Company's truck and apparently a fair load to deliver. I watched him drive up slowly from round the corner by the emporium, moving as though he were going to a funeral. I expect his engine was playing up with it being such a devilish cold morning. Then he got the ice block out from under the tarpaulin sheeting, wrapped in felt, and took it to the shop window.'

'Wrapped in felt?' Denning looked curious. 'But didn't he use the usual grapples — or whatever they call 'em?'

'No sir. Apparently used the felt instead to prevent the block slipping. Didn't seem to me that there was anything suspicious about it.'

'And you are sure no attempts were made to enter the property during the night?'

'Yes. Nothing happened while I was on duty.'

'So says Saunders. I had a word with him on the way back from the ruins. He's perfectly convinced that there was no hidden object in the Bilkin place when he examined it yesterday, nor, during his spell of duty, did he see anybody suspicious knocking about.' Denning became thoughtful. 'Did you see the ice this man was carrying? I mean, did you see it *clearly*?'

'Yes sir. When he arrived I hadn't taken up position in the alley. I was only two doors away.'

'Was the ice transparent? Could you see light through it?'

'Fairly well, where the felt didn't cover it.' P.C. Marsden's eyes gleamed. 'You're wondering if perhaps something was concealed in the ice block, sir? I'm sure there wasn't. It would have shown up darkly against the light and I never saw anything like that. Being on the job I watched with especial keenness.'

Denning nodded and gave a little sigh. 'All right, Marsden. Get off home and take a rest. You've had a pretty rough time of it.'

'Thank you, sir.' P.C. Marsden picked up his helmet, and left the office. Grant looked at his superior questioningly.

'*Did* you think there might be something in the ice, sir?' he asked.

'Matter of fact, yes — though I suppose it's crazy. I'm fishing round for ways to explain how some sort of — of infernal machine got into that shop. Inside an ice block would be unusual, but perhaps possible.'

'Unless it happened to be an electrical device,' Grant said, with his usual tendency to look below the surface. 'That would mean first standing it in water, which was afterwards made into the ice block — and no matter how well sealed the device it wouldn't improve its electrical powers. Anyway, the Cold Ice Company is highly reputable. Why should they want to blow up Bilkin's place?'

Denning said: 'The Old Boy isn't going to like this one little bit. Well, you'd better get off to Werton with that note, Grant, and then — Come in,' he sighed, and this time the sergeant-in-charge of the outer office ushered in the dapper, precise Amos Ballam, the fire assessor.

'You wanted me to call, Superintendent?' he asked politely, taking off his bowler hat to reveal neatly brushed grey hair.

'That's right, Mr. Ballam. Have a seat.' Denning returned to his swivel-chair at the desk and considered him pensively. 'I take it that you have now investigated the ruins of Mr. Bilkin's shop?'

'As thoroughly as possible considering the heat still lying in those ashes. I'll make another survey later. This is purely the preliminary — hem! — once-over.'

'I see. Did you find any explanation for the explosion and fire?'

'At this stage I didn't expect to, but at least I'm satisfied enough to recommend

Mrs. Bilkin to make out her claim — to which I shall give my personal attention.'

'Mr. Bilkin mentioned that he had had an insurance policy with the Paragon Company for the past fifteen years. Do you know if it covered all eventualities?'

'Oh, you mean fully comprehensive! Unfortunately, no.' The assessor brooded over this fact and did not seem particularly pleased about it either. 'If that were so my task would be a good deal easier. However, there it is.'

Denning jotted down the facts and nodded. 'Thanks, Mr. Ballam. I suppose the Paragon will send an assessor of their own to check on your findings?'

Ballam gave a cold smile. 'They have that weakness,' he conceded. 'The Paragon's man will be here within a few hours of my claim reaching them — which will be by registered mail this evening. I expect he will turn up some time tomorrow.'

'I understand. Well, I don't need to detain you further, sir.'

Amos Ballam got to his feet, said 'Good day' with studied politeness, and departed.

'Just as I said, sir,' Grant observed. 'Even if there *is* something phony Ballam isn't the man to say so. Anyway, I'll be getting off to Werton.'

Denning sat thinking after his subordinate had left the office. As a policeman he had to examine all possibilities. Had the disaster been planned skilfully in order to collect the insurance monies? But what made the theory shaky were the fatal injuries Bilkin himself had sustained in the execution of the plot.

Oscar Bilkin himself had surely not been responsible for the explosion — unless his own death had been an unforeseeable accident. And as for the buxom wife or cheery daughter planning such a thing . . .

'I don't believe it,' Denning muttered, taking up the telephone to give his report to the Chief Constable — better known as the 'Old Boy'.

He completed his telephone report and then feeling quite annoyed with himself left the office and went out to his car. In ten minutes it had taken him to the Halingford General Hospital and he was conducted to the ward where, in beds next to each other, Mrs. Bilkin and her daughter were lying Neither of them was severely hurt — so the doctor explained to Denning — but they needed watching for a day or two.

Denning found them apparently normal though sombre with the gravity of events. They propped themselves up in their respective beds as he settled on a chair between them and took off his uniform cap.

'I am hoping, ladies,' he said, sitting so that his back was not turned to either of them, 'that you'll be able to shed some light on this terrible business. As a man I can only express my condolences to both you and your daughter — but as a policeman I can — and will — leave nothing unturned until I have found out who *caused* the death of Mr. Bilkin.'

'You mean his murder, Superintendent, don't you?' Edith Bilkin asked sharply, and Denning glanced at her. Her voice was curt, her visible brown eye challenging. The other eye was obscured by wadding. 'Dad was *murdered* — just as Mum and I might have been if we hadn't been lucky. Somebody had it in for all of us — and the business — and I'd like to get my hands on them!'

'I can understand that, Miss Bilkin, but it's a matter for the law,' Denning responded. 'You can best help by telling me everything you know. In the first place, did any of you happen to notice the smell of gas before the explosion?'

'I didn't,' Mrs. Bilkin said flatly. 'But then, I can't smell much at any time.'

Denning felt, most irrelevantly, that this was perhaps the explanation for her tolerating the fish business. 'And you, Miss Bilkin?' he asked.

'There was no smell of gas whatever,' she answered firmly. 'Besides, even supposing there had been a lot of gas, it would have had to collect in one space, wouldn't it? It couldn't have done that in the kitchen because there was a big fire. Then again the shop door was opened to let P.C. Marsden in for a cup of tea. After that I opened the window for the ice. If there'd been any gas it would have escaped, wouldn't it?'

'Yes, it would,' Denning agreed. 'Let us consider the note, then. I understand it arrived by post around noon yesterday, and your father was the first person to find it?'

'He was,' Mrs. Bilkin said, as her daughter nodded. 'We'd just had dinner and he was going to open the shop for the afternoon. At the time I thought the whole thing was a joke. Now I wish to 'eaven I hadn't been so cocksure about it. Somebody knew what was coming and whoever that person was did it.'

'That somebody knew what was coming is certainly true,' Denning assented. 'But it's most unlikely that that person caused the tragedy. He — or she — would hardly warn you to get out of the place when the apparent object was to kill all three of you. It would defeat its own purpose.'

'But suppose, Superintendent,' Mrs. Bilkin said, pondering, 'whoever it was did that to give us a chance to get out, the real intention being to just blow the shop up?'

'That is a theory I had already formed, Mrs. Bilkin. Can you think of anybody, likely or unlikely, who might have the slightest wish to do so?'

'I can't,' Mrs. Bilkin said at length. 'We haven't — or hadn't — any big competitors in Halingford; no multiple store-owners selling fish and vegetables like us, who might have wanted to get us out of the way.'

'The problem,' Denning went on, 'is to decide how the explosion was caused. We may bring some definite facts to light when the ashes have cooled enough for police fire-experts to make an examination, but until then valuable time may be lost. The only caller before the explosion was, I believe, the ice-man?'

'That's right,' Edith nodded. 'Not the usual chap, though. Usually it's Bill Higgins who brings the ice, but this new chap said Bill had been transferred to another round. Didn't look as though this chap knew the job very well, either. He handled the ice like a baby instead of a block of frozen water — '

'Yes,' Denning interposed. 'According to P.C. Marsden the ice was delivered wrapped in felt?'

'Almost, yes,' Edith agreed. 'The felt was wrapped round the sides and the ends were left free. Perhaps the felt was so that he could keep a grip on the block. He didn't use the tongs, like Bill Higgins usually does.'

'Was it just your particular ice-block which was wrapped in felt?'

'The remainder of the blocks were covered by tarpaulin,' Edith explained. 'This chap must be a lot more careful than Bill Higgins. *He* never went to all that trouble. Our one block had the felt round it — far as I know.'

'And I believe the truck approached your shop very slowly?' Denning questioned.

'That's right. The chap told me it was engine trouble.'

'I see. And the ice was delivered by the quite reputable firm of the Cold Ice Company?'

'Nothing wrong with *them*!' Mrs. Bilkin declared. 'Dealt with 'em for years.'

'About what time did he arrive?' Denning asked.

'Quarter past seven,' Edith replied. 'Three quarters of an hour earlier than usual.'

'The ice, I take it, was used for the fish?'

'Yes,' said Edith. 'Dad used to break it up with a hammer and chisel and then put the fish slices on a sort of ice carpet.'

'Did either of you see the ice at close quarters?' Denning asked.

'I did,' Edith said. 'But there was nothing wrong with the ice, if that's what you mean — except that it looked a bit dirty. Yellowish. Dad said it was perhaps some preservative in the water.'

'Why preservative in ice-water?' Denning frowned. 'It was entirely transparent, I suppose? You could see right through it?'

Edith looked surprised. 'Of course! You always can through ice, can't you?'

Denning had the feeling he was flogging a dead horse. From two sources he had now verified that the ice had been transparent and had nothing hidden inside it. He switched tack.

'When the explosion occurred, just what happened?'

'Kitchen fell in on me,' said Mrs. Bilkin. 'I was just layin' out the breakfast when the wall between the kitchen and the shop came straight at me. The ceiling came down too . . . Somehow I was thrown under the kitchen table and everything came tumbling down on top of it. I couldn't get free, and had to wait for help.'

'I was blown out of the back of the van in the yard,' Edith said. 'Something hit me over the eye and I crashed into the wall. It knocked me silly. Next thing I knew I was in the ambulance.'

'I see . . . I understand the place was insured, Mrs. Bilkin?'

'We insured it fifteen years ago, with the Paragon Company. It was my hubby's idea after we'd had one of those pushin' salesmen after us. Thought we might as well — and thank 'eaven we did. This lot has cleaned us out — except for what's in the bank, of course. I asked the hospital to telephone to Mr. Ballam. He's going to assess the — '

Denning interrupted with the assurance that he had already done his job, and then added a few details to make the position plain. Finally he added gravely:

'I don't want to throw cold water at a time like this, Mrs. Bilkin, but I'd say it is most unlikely that the insurance company will pay up.'

6

Blank consternation settled on Mrs. Bilkin's face, and she gave her daughter an anxious glance. 'Why not?' she demanded. 'They're a perfectly reliable company.'

'I'm sure they will contest the claim on the ground that it was not an accident but a deliberate effort at arson — and perhaps murder, though that part will not concern them as much. I'm sure Mr. Ballam will do all he can, but the policy was not completely comprehensive — meaning that it didn't guard you against every possible accident. Added to that is the fact that the press will carry the news of the note your husband received, which in itself should be sufficient to cause any insurance company to withhold payment — at least pending intense investigation.'

'But . . . ' Mrs. Bilkin was genuinely bewildered. 'Does the press have to know about that note?'

'It's difficult to prevent the facts leaking out. Your husband told me he went to several people with it before he came to me. And again, your shop had police protection. Those sort of facts get about. The men your husband visited will have talked — following the explosion. On top of that there will be an inquest on your husband and the facts will have to come out. What will finally cap it will be my asking for an adjournment of the inquest pending police enquiry. I'm afraid,' Denning finished, smiling seriously, 'that your hopes of a settlement, less agent's fee, are a bit shaky, Mrs. Bilkin.'

The women were obviously stunned, and Denning regretted that he had had to appear so ruthless. However, it had given him the chance to see the reaction of the two women to the prospect of losing the insurance money.

From what he saw now of expressions and manner he decided that Mrs. Bilkin had nothing to do with the business. Nor the daughter. The girl had become moodily silent, but it was not the silence of bitter disgust — but of completely shattering disappointment.

'Did you see anybody strange — apart from the usual run of Halingford people — about the shop or main street either yesterday or the day before?' Denning asked. 'Whoever blew your place up might have studied it carefully from outside to weigh up some kind of plan. Unless the person did it from inside a van or car he — or she — must have been more or less visible.'

Mrs. Bilkin pondered. 'Come to think of it, I *did* see somebody who I haven't seen for eight years or more! What's more,' the woman went on, 'he spent quite a bit of time staring at our shop from across the street. It was late on last Monday afternoon. We'd closed the shop by then and I was tidying up while Ozzy was in the kitchen going through his invoices. This chap came out of Hunter's teashop across the road from us. He looked as if he was studying the neighbourhood. Then he walked on up the road.'

'Was he a stranger?' Denning asked sharply.

'Yes and no. More of a prodigal, you might say. It was Mr. Drew — Gordon Drew. Son of old Mr. Arthur Drew who used to own one of those big houses in Sundale Avenue.'

'Where Dr. Carruthers now lives,' the superintendent said; and though he had already met Gordon Drew he did not mention the fact.

'Dr. Carruthers has it now,' Mrs. Bilkin agreed, 'but years ago Mr. Drew senior had it — and then a tea merchant. Anyway, Mr. Drew senior had a good-for-nothing son who never did any work. Then the family left the district — eight years ago. The other afternoon young Gordon came back to town again. I'd know him anywhere. Only thing different about him is that he looked a good deal older, naturally, and he seemed to have got a scar on his cheek from somewhere.'

'That's very interesting, Mrs. Bilkin. Can you think of any reason why Mr. Drew might want to make trouble for you?'

The woman shrugged fleshy shoulders. 'His people used to deal with us for fish and vegetables and as far as I know were quite satisfied.'

'How was he dressed that afternoon?'

'Oh, he had on a heavy topcoat and no hat. Dark-haired, and about five feet ten.'

'Thanks.' Denning was satisfied it was the same Gordon Drew. He got to his feet. 'I won't bother you any more today, ladies. Oh, where will you be going when you leave the hospital? I'll have to contact you to attend the inquest, of course, providing you've recovered sufficiently.'

'We're going to my sister's in Larch Avenue for the time being,' Mrs. Bilkin replied. 'Number twenty-two.'

'Right,' Denning nodded. 'I'll be on my way — and I hope you'll both soon be better.'

Returning to his car, he did not switch on the ignition immediately: instead he sat pondering. He was reasonably satisfied that the creator of the fish-shop disaster had not been either Mrs. Bilkin or her daughter.

Definitely interesting was the fact that a one-time inhabitant of Halingford had returned and surveyed the shop with more than average interest. And now he was secretary to Dr. Carruthers — but to Superintendent Denning, Gordon Drew had now become a possible suspect in the business, and as such had to be investigated.

Since Detective-Sergeant Grant would not yet be back from Werton, Denning decided to call on the proprietor of the teashop where, according to Mrs. Bilkin, Drew had called. He started the car engine and drove back into the centre of the town.

The windows of the teashop had been blown out, he noticed, and much of the paint on the door and window-frame had been blistered by the heat of the fire.

By some fluke the florist's next door had escaped damage in so far that though cracked by heat the windows had not been broken. Here too the paint was a mass of blisters.

The florist did not seem to be concerned enough about the damage to protect his window with strips of sticky paper: the tea-shop proprietor on the other hand was busily nailing plywood into position as the superintendent got out of his car and walked across the pavement. He could have spoken through the smashed opening but preferred the greater privacy of the shop itself.

The proprietor laid aside his hammer and edged along behind the confectionery counter enquiringly. '"Morning, Inspector,' he smiled tautly. 'Come about that rotten business over the way, eh?'

'Partly,' Denning conceded; 'but actually I'm interested in a man who apparently called in here late on Monday afternoon. A tallish chap in a heavy overcoat and not wearing a hat. Dark-haired and young.'

'Oh, *him*! He had tea and biscuits, and asked a lot of questions.'

'What sort of questions, exactly?'

'"Bout everybody, more or less.' The proprietor frowned thoughtfully. 'I couldn't make out whether he was just plain nosy or up to something. Mind you, he did say he hadn't been in this town for eight years, so I suppose he was sort of refreshing his memory. He asked a lot of things — if there was a family called Lloyd — the

Borough Surveyor, you know; and if his daughter was still in the district. I told him yes, of course.'

'Go on,' Denning invited, interested.

'Then he asked if old Bilkin was still alive, and if there was anybody new around here. Only person I could think of was my next-door neighbour — Bedford, the florist. I told him I hadn't much time for florist's and he came out with a funny sort of remark . . . something about needing a wreath when you die.'

'Anything else?'

'Oh yes, he asked if the emporium across the way was new. I told him it was. He looked a bit of a suspicious sort of card to me — had a burn scar on his face. Put me in mind of a pirate. What's he done, anyway? Blown up Bilkin's place?'

'Don't let ideas like that run away with you,' Denning warned him. 'Thanks for what you've told me — and remember it's confidential.'

'If you say so,' the proprietor agreed, and Denning left him and returned to his car.

It was still but eleven o'clock, so there

was a chance that Miss Lloyd, the daughter of the Borough Surveyor, might be at home. Drew had enquired after her — according to the teashop proprietor — so it was possible she might be able to provide some sidelight on the prodigal.

Denning drove along the main street towards the residential section where the Georgian home of the Lloyds was situated.

* * *

In the depths of the dispensary in Granwell's Emporium, Stuart Jones was working by himself, nor was he particularly pleased with the responsibility — but since Clayton Ross had not put in his usual appearance that morning there was nothing else for it.

Dispensing chemists do not grow on trees and to find an assistant at a moment's notice was beyond the powers of the great Granwell — even if he had chosen to exert them on behalf of the overworked employee.

Jones had reported Ross's absence to

the emporium's general manager and he in turn had reported by devious slaves to the Presence when he had arrived in his office at the top of the building towards ten-fifteen. From that point onwards nothing more had happened and Stuart Jones was thus left to cope with things as best he could.

The explosion at Bilkin's fish-shop had occurred a full hour and a half before any of the employees of the emporium had put in an appearance for work at ten to nine. Tempting though the sight of smoke, fire brigade, ambulance and police had been for all of them, the haunting vision of the ruthless Boss had forced them reluctantly past the spot and so to work — Stuart Jones amongst them.

And now Jones was wondering if Clayton Ross, with some crackpot idea in his head, had taken the morning off to watch the proceedings at the fish-shop disaster.

Jones was left to wonder what he ought to do about it. Work kept coming in from the upper regions, increasing into a steadily mounting pile of prescriptions through which he could not possibly wade without putting in a good deal of overtime. It was too much to expect any one man to accomplish.

Then the matter seemed as if it were going to be settled for him, for towards half past eleven he was summoned to the office of the All Highest.

He took the self-service lift to the top of the building. A few yards down a soft-carpeted corridor was a glass-panelled office door with an imposing — RUPERT GRANWELL, MANAGING DIRECTOR executed upon it.

Jones knocked lightly, winced at the brief 'Come in!' — and entered. Despite the cloudy mystery in which he chose to move there was nothing whatever ethereal about Rupert Granwell, and he conformed more or less to the whispered descriptions of him which circulated from time to time.

He was stout, pink-faced, with brown hair rather similar in curls and colour to that of an imitation mohair rug. When presently he looked up from the correspondence he had been studying it was with a fixed, stern glare from small grey-blue eyes.

'Ross come yet?' he demanded.

'No, sir, I'm afraid he hasn't.' The chinless Jones was quiet and respectful.

'And why the devil not?'

'I've no idea, sir. I've been wondering about it all morning.'

'Wondering! Huh! I don't pay you to wonder: I pay you to work. See that you do! It's a damned nuisance . . . We'll be getting behind with orders and prescriptions in the drugs department if we don't do something.'

Jones realized the big man's mind was more concerned with losing business than in helping out an overworked employee.

'But,' Granwell added, 'I can't find a head dispenser in a few minutes, and you yourself are by no means suitable for the job. Besides, I don't know what has happened to Ross. He may be ill, in which case my hands are tied. Did he say give any intimation that he might be away? You work with him.'

'He did say recently that he was getting very dissatisfied . . . sir. He was thinking of either quitting his job or asking you to get us larger quarters than our present dispensary. I didn't altogether agree with him but for the sake of peace I didn't say too much. We do have to work together . . . ' Jones' voice trailed off and became silent.

Rupert Granwell merely gazed — with terrifying power.

'Which means,' Jones interpreted hastily, 'that he may have walked out. Always full of swollen ideas about controlling things for himself instead of having an employer. Now with me it's different, I know my place — '

'What's *wrong* with your quarters?' Granwell interrupted. 'They conform to regulations because they've got to!'

'I'm perfectly satisfied, sir — but Ross isn't, or wasn't.'

'Then why the devil couldn't he have come and done it himself? He's the head dispenser and entitled to air his grievances — within limits.'

'But . . . ' Jones hesitated over the glorious thought that he had perhaps caught Clayton Ross out at last. 'I understood that he *did* come and see you, sir — the evening before last. At any rate, he left the dispensary with the full resolve to do so.'

'It's three weeks since I've seen Ross,' Granwell replied. 'About what time was he supposed to come and see me?'

'It was exactly five-thirty. He deliberately waited until then because he thought it would be his best opportunity to catch you alone. He wasn't away long and when he came back he didn't say anything about his interview, so I assumed you'd turned down his suggestions. You see, sir, his expression looked so queer, as though he'd had a row — a wiping down. That could only have been from you.'

'Sort of — frightened?' Granwell hazarded.

'Yes — I'd never seen him look that way before. From the look on his face I just didn't dare ask him how he'd got on, somehow.'

Awkward silence — then Granwell seemed to make up his mind about something.

‘I’ll get in touch with his rooms, Jones. If he’s walked out without notice I’ll arrange for somebody to take his place.’

‘Very good, sir.’ Stuart Jones summoned up unsuspected courage. ‘You — you don’t think I might do his job with an assistant to help me? I’m qualified.’

‘I’ll think about it,’ Granwell said absently, and with this Stuart Jones had for the time being to be satisfied.

7

It was about two-thirty when Dr. Carruthers and Gordon Drew found their respective activities in connection with the book on atomic physics disturbed by visitors.

As far as Gordon was concerned the interruption was welcome for the housekeeper ushered in Janice Lloyd, in her smart two-piece and saucy hat, and then the tall, quiet figure of Superintendent Denning, in his official uniform.

Carruthers, seated at his desk, his mane of hair more untidy than ever, looked up sharply and then in wonder.

'Well, I'll be damned!' he exclaimed frankly, getting to his feet. 'How are you, Miss Lloyd? Glad to see you again.' He shook hands and switched his piercing blue eyes to Denning. 'What's your reason, Denning? Not because you're feeling romantic towards Mr. Drew here, of course?'

The elephantine humour failed to register. The superintendent gave a reserved little smile and Janice flushed slightly at the scientist's impish glance in her direction.

'Well, sit down,' Carruthers invited. 'I don't know what this is all about, and frankly it's most inconvenient, but you may as well be comfortable.'

When they had all settled in chairs round the fire Denning opened the conversation. 'Sorry for breaking in on you like this, Dr. Carruthers, only it's rather important.'

'Got yourself tied in knots with this Bilkin explosion?' Carruthers asked dryly.

'No, sir. I just want a few words with you, Mr. Drew . . . privately.'

'What about?' Gordon opened his grey eyes wide.

'That, sir, is confidential. And — er — ' Denning added, with a glance at the girl — 'it seems that the proprietor of the teashop in Halingford Road, where you had tea the other day, remembered you asking after Miss Lloyd, I felt she might know something about you so I called upon her and she insisted on bringing me here. I'd like you to come down to the station, Mr. Drew, for a chat.'

Gordon shook his head calmly. 'Sorry, Superintendent. I'm quite aware that you're following legal procedure in wishing to interview me in private — but there's nothing Dr. Carruthers shouldn't know — or Miss Lloyd either. So, fire away.'

'As you wish,' Denning shrugged. 'I've been having a chat with Mrs. Bilkin, and there is one point upon which I'd like you to enlarge, What is — or rather was — your interest in the Bilkin shop? Why were you so interested in the Bilkin family as to ask the teashop proprietor all about them?'

'Why was I — ?' Sheer amazement stopped Gordon Drew for a moment; then he grinned. 'Ye gods! Are you trying to tie me up with *that* business this morning?'

'I have to examine every angle,' Denning said patiently, quite undisturbed. 'I'd like you to answer the question.'

'With pleasure.' Gordon Drew gave a whimsical little smile. 'It's simply that I'm what you might call an old boy round this district. I used to live in this very house — eight years ago. Miss Lloyd will verify that, as will Dr. Carruthers. I was just reviving a few old memories and discovering how many of the old faces are still in existence. Anybody is liable to do that, returning to a home town after an interval of years.'

'I believe you also wanted to know about the teashop proprietor's next door neighbour?'

'Not at all. He volunteered the information. I was interested, though, because the shop used to be Baxter's where I bought all manner of gadgets for my bike.'

'I believe you spent quite a few minutes studying Mr. Bilkin's shop when you left the teashop?'

'Yes — but I didn't give it my exclusive attention, I was simply surveying the High Street as a whole and noting, if you must know, that Mr. Bilkin seemed to be about the only survivor of the old days, on that side of the road. I thought of having a word with Mrs. Bilkin, whom I could see in the shop, but I changed my mind in favour of looking for Janice.'

Silence, then: 'What in blue thunder do you mean by questioning this boy in such a fashion?' Carruthers growled

'Merely following up a lead, Doctor,' Denning replied guardedly.

'Lead be damned! I wouldn't have taken him on as my assistant if I hadn't been satisfied as to his integrity! You're wasting time here — including mine, dammit.'

Denning remained unfazed, and turned again to Gordon.

'I take it then, sir, that it was nothing else but nostalgia which brought you back to Halingford?'

'What else? One would hardly return here for the sake of viewing the scenery — as such. I'd lost most of my money, had had enough of wandering from place to place and felt in the mood for reviving old memories. Also — I freely admit it — I wanted to renew my acquaintance with Miss Lloyd.'

'I understand.' Denning got to his feet and smiled reservedly. 'Since you were the only person seen scrutinizing the Bilkin property with a more than normal interest it demanded looking into — and has had it. I'm working on the hypothesis that whoever plotted to blow up Bilkin's place must have studied the building beforehand.'

'And must then have got the infernal machine — or whatever it was — into the building,' Carruthers pointed out. 'I can vouch for it that this young man here did not do that. From becoming my secretary on Monday night until now, except for a few minutes this morning when he accidentally met Miss Lloyd — he has not left these premises.'

'A guarantee that I accept, sir,' Denning acknowledged. 'And thank you — all of you.' He turned to leave, but before he had reached the door Carruthers called him back

'Look here, Denning, why don't you share your troubles?' he suggested, rising from the armchair. 'This business with Bilkin has got you stopped dead, hasn't it?'

'Not yet, sir. A great deal of time hasn't elapsed yet. I have many lines of enquiry to follow.' There was modest assurance in the superintendent's tone.

'You have, eh?' Carruthers looked more like Beethoven than ever, as he stood peering up at Denning curiously. 'But if you get stuck and feel tempted to call in the lads of Scotland Yard — which will not enhance *your* reputation — think of me instead. You've got possibilities: I'll help you if I can.'

'I'll remember that, Doctor, thanks,' Denning answered. 'I admit hard to see how the cause of the explosion was introduced into the fish-shop . . . '

No brilliant theories came from Carruthers. He merely turned and dug out a buried teapot from the desk top, poured a watery stream into a cup perched on top of a textbook.

'Mind you,' Carruthers said, pouring milk into the cup and then tossing in a saccharin tablet, 'if I help you it doesn't mean that I've any intention of running about like a policeman, looking for clues. I've no time for such things, but I will be able to give you the reactions of an observant man who is accustomed to assessing the scientific implications of a problem.'

'Yes, sir, I'm sure of it,' Denning smiled. 'Thanks again.'

He went out and closed the door. Carruthers swallowed the half-cup of tepid tea and set it down with a decisive hand. 'Confident young pup,' he muttered.

'Nice of him to pick on me, anyway,' Gordon Drew commented sourly.

Carruthers shrugged. 'He simply happens to be good at his work that's all — but good though he may be, overflowing with cocksureness — he's up against something tough. I think he's going to find that whoever did the Bilkin trick not only knows all the answers but the questions as well.'

'Father's dreadfully upset about the whole affair,' Janice remarked. 'As Borough Surveyor, the destruction of the fish-shop has upset his town planning scheme, or something. I don't quite understand it properly, but at lunch he was talking about a complete revaluation of the property round Halingford Road.'

Carruthers did not comment, but he seemed to be thinking. The girl looked at Gordon as he still frowned.

'I hope I did right in bringing the superintendent here? I didn't want to answer any of his questions without you hearing me.'

'Of course,' Gordon smiled at her. 'I've nothing to hide.'

'Complete revaluation of Halingford Road property, you said Miss Lloyd?' Carruthers mused.

'Why, yes.' The girl turned to him again. 'But that's only the gist of what Dad said — and he didn't elaborate either. In fact I got the impression he was sorry he said anything at all. It sort of — slipped out.'

'Mmmm,' Carruthers said, then with a grin which had an edge of reproof in it, he added: 'Neither of you seem to understand the meaning of business hours! It happened this morning, and it's happening again now. It won't do! Gordon, save up your conversation with

Miss Lloyd for your spare time.'

'I'll go,' Janice said, taking the hint. 'Let me know when you've some spare time.'

She left the Den and closed the door — and at about this time a very perplexed superintendent was entering the police station.

It was the first time he had returned here since departing for the hospital in the morning — his dinner he had had at his rooms — and in response to his enquiry of the sergeant-in-charge as to whether Grant had returned he was told he was in his office.

He was earnestly reading through a pile of newspapers, but he got to his feet as his superior came in.

'Well, Grant, how did you get on?' Denning asked.

'Fair to middling, sir,' Grant replied, pulling from his wallet the official forensic report from Werton. 'Both the notepaper and envelope of that warning are a mass of different fingerprints, so it's impossible to get anything from them. They are both of the ordinary cheap variety that anybody could buy, so there is not much there to help us. No watermark or anything. The other point is that seven newspapers were used to get the message together.'

'Seven?' Denning looked surprised.

'So say the experts,' Grant shrugged. 'Their analysis shows seven different varieties of newsprint in all the letters out of which the warning and the address were made. What I'm doing now, sir, is going through these seven leading daily papers which I bought in Werton. I've already traced where some of the 'cut out' letters came from — sub-headlines chiefly. I had difficulty getting hold of the papers, by the way, because they're yesterday's. I didn't *know* they would be: I risked it. And it came off. That at least tells us something — that the warning note was not prepared before yesterday.'

Denning smiled. The information supported his belief that the detective-sergeant was a man who could act effectively on his own inclination.

'When I've ranged up all seven papers, sir, we might have something to go on,' Grant added. 'We shall know from which papers the note was produced.'

'After which,' Denning said, discarding his uniform cap and settling at the desk, 'the logical course of enquiry is to question the newsagents in and around this district. It's unlikely that any one person would have seven morning newspapers as a regular thing.'

'So I think,' Grant agreed. 'It's also unlikely that the person concerned would be fool enough to buy all seven papers at one shop. Draw too much attention — but there is the possibility that he bought one each at seven different shops. If then we make enquiry and find a certain customer is repeated in description by at least three out of seven newsagents we can be pretty sure it tallies with the description of the person who prepared the note.'

'Yes, we can try it,' Denning agreed, thinking. 'Trouble is, newsagents are busy people, especially in the morning, and I don't think much store can be placed on their powers of observation concerning one customer in particular. Just the same we'll see what we can do. I'll give you a hand to trace the newspapers we want.'

This task took them a little over an hour, but finally they had identified the various small type headlines from which the original words had been built up, and on the detective-sergeant's notepad were the names of seven regular dailies.

'I thought it couldn't be evening papers, sir, because there aren't that many circulate round this district,' he explained. 'Only morning newspapers seemed to fill the bill. At any rate, that's that!' He gave a little nod of satisfaction. 'If you wish I'll start the job of enquiry right away — before the newsagents have a chance to completely forget.'

'Right — do that.' Denning got to his feet and retrieved the warning and envelope.

'How far did you manage to get, sir?' Grant asked, as he prepared to depart. 'See Mrs. Bilkin and the girl?'

'I saw them all right, and I also saw Gordon Drew again . . . Dr. Carruthers' new secretary. I can't make head or tail of that chap! He's a sort of negative character . . . just doesn't assert himself in any way, and yet you can't help being aware of his presence. Anyway, I gathered a few facts.' Denning outlined what had occurred and the story left the detective-sergeant thoughtful.

'Which doesn't seem to get us much further, sir,' he commented. 'Unless you've any ideas of your own?'

'I wish I had,' Denning sighed. 'Two things have got me stumped — first, the motive for such a senseless, brutal crime; and second, how it was done. In regard to the first, the facts will only come to light as we progress further; but as regards the second I can do something right away — and I'm going to. I'm having the best man in the fire department examine those ruins in detail for any clue that he can find which might explain matters, before the insurance company's assessor arrives tomorrow. Between them they ought surely to dig out some sort of explanation. Then we'll go further. One thing I'm sure about, though — Mrs. and Miss Bilkin are blameless. They get nothing out of the whole business except hard luck'

'And this chap Gordon Drew? You believe him?'

Denning shrugged. 'No reason not to. He had nostalgia, came back to look the district over, paid attention to landmarks familiar to him — and finished up by getting a job with Dr Carruthers. Miss Lloyd told me how he got that: Carruthers took a fancy to him because he leaned on the railing outside his place. Just about the eccentric thing that vest-pocket mastermind would do! The story holds together, and it will have to do until I have something more to lead the attack again. You see, Grant, for all we know Drew may have had other reasons for coming back to town, and the elimination of Bilkin might have been one of them. Pure guesswork, though.'

'At least it's something to chew over,' Grant said.

'Drew's very appearance is against him,' Denning muttered, reflecting. 'There's a big burn scar he has on his face that gives him an unexpectedly criminal aspect.'

'Can't judge by that, sir,' Grant said stolidly. 'It's axiomatic that a criminal doesn't often look like one.'

'I agree. But I am entitled to wonder at a man having a severe burn scar and then an explosion and a fire breaks out mysteriously within a few hours of him arriving in Halingford. Anyhow, Grant, go and see about those newspapers and report back later. I'll be staying behind this evening. Next thing we'll have the Old Boy down here wanting to know what we're doing — so I must get the facts — such as they are — sorted in readiness.'

8

Before the grey light of the short February day had faded Superintendent Denning went into action, and by four o'clock, accompanied by the chief of the Halingford fire brigade — Brewster by name, a square, solid individual who had made fires and their causes — and their extinguishing — his sole passion in life — he was exploring the now cooled ruins of the Bilkin shop.

He and the fire chief worked to a systematic plan, moving inwards from the outer perimeter of the fire towards the centre. In this way, moving foot by foot and turning over the charred ashes with long iron rods borrowed from the fire station, they did not miss a single inch of debris.

But, though they found bits of bent metal here and there, melted lead piping elsewhere, the warped remains of a kitchen range, several fire-blasted taps and a blackened bath — they came across nothing really untoward, nothing even remotely suggestive of the exploded 'innards' of an infernal machine.

Denning waited until Brewster had completed his examination and the afternoon was paling into twilight — then he glanced at him enquiringly.

'Well, Brewster, what have we got out of this?'

'Nothing, Super, unless of course there is something buried deep down, blown a long way into the ground by the force of the explosion. Such things can happen, but it's pretty unlikely in this case.' Brewster's keen eyes studied the drunkenly leaning walls of the half-shattered neighbouring buildings. 'From the direction of the blast, the whole thing began as a powerful explosion — but there we stop. There don't seem to be any bits of metal such as might have belonged to a home-made bomb.'

'How about gas?' Denning asked. 'That cause it?'

'It could,' Brewster agreed dubiously, 'but unignited gas in sufficient cubic density to cause such a terrific explosion would have been noticeable by its odour. Besides, it wouldn't be sealed in. Windows and doors, unless taped — and fireplace flues — would allow it to dissipate.'

Denning nodded moodily. No, gas was not the answer. He recalled that Edith Bilkin had denied she'd smelled any gas. And the front door had been opened, first to the constable and then to the ice-man. The window had been pushed up to allow the ice to be put on the slab. Besides, there had been a fire in the kitchen . . .

'Well, Brewster, this is all we can do,' he said finally, turning away from the debris. 'Thanks for your help.'

'You're welcome,' the fire chief responded. 'When these ashes are dead cold I'll have them carted away and sifted, and we can also search again. If there is anything buried deep down we'll find it.'

'Right,' Denning said. 'I'll hope for that, then.'

They parted — Denning down the main street to the police station and Brewster to his car.

The superintendent returned to his headquarters to find that Grant had not yet arrived back with the results of the newsagents' comb-out. He had some tea sent in and pondered while he slowly consumed it.

The chief stumbling block was the lack of motive. Denning was beginning to think that he was being called upon to solve something impossible — yet if he admitted this fact to Colonel Barrow, the Chief Constable, when he turned up to see how things were going, it would probably mean calling in the Yard.

'And down will go my stock!' Denning muttered. 'I'll solve it if it kills me!'

Following a tap on the door, Detective-Sergeant Grant came in.

'I think we have something, sir,' he said, coming straight to the point. 'As you know, there are six major newsagents in the town, and I've been to all of them. Three couldn't remember anything at all, then at the fourth shop I got a lead. The chap remembers a fellow buying two newspapers yesterday morning early — two, sir; note that. He gave me his description. At the fifth and sixth shops I was ready armed with this description and the newsagents seem to have a hazy recollection of such a man buying a newspaper, but they can't recall which paper. From that I think we're entitled to infer that the chap who bought two newspapers at one shop — there being seven newspapers and only six shops he could have gone to — might be worth interviewing.'

'Not very good grounds, Grant. I buy two newspapers myself sometimes.'

Grant smiled. He had kept the succulent part until last.

'I found out the chap's name, from the newsagents where the two newspapers were bought. He said quite unhesitatingly that it was a chap named Ross. He's the head dispenser at Granwell's Emporium across the road and buys a single paper at that shop every morning. This time he was earlier than usual and bought two.'

'And it's more or less possible that the same chap went to the other shops?' Denning asked sharply.

'From the description I'd say yes.'

'Then what are we waiting for?' The superintendent jumped to his feet and glanced at the clock. 'Quarter to six. We've just time to get some information from the emporium. Come on.'

They left the police station hurriedly but slowed to a walk more becoming to the dignity of the law as they saw that Granwell's Emporium was still open across the street, its windows brilliantly lighted.

Once within its warm, expansive wilderness, which had the quietness of ten minutes prior to closing time, a shopwalker directed the two men to Rupert Granwell's sanctum.

He was absorbed in the evening edition of the *Halingford Gazette* but tossed it on one side and got to his feet as the two men were shown into his office.

'Well, gentlemen, good evening.' He shook hands. 'Not that I like having the law invading my premises. Makes the staff talk.'

'It concerns one of your employees,' Denning said quietly. 'Since you are the managing director of the firm I must acquaint you with my intentions. I'd like to speak to your head dispenser, Mr. Ross — privately.'

Granwell motioned them to chairs. 'Ross no longer works here. I'm replacing him at the earliest moment. In fact I have an advertisement in tonight's *Gazette* here.'

Denning frowned. 'You mean that you have discharged him?'

'No. He walked out on me.' His eyes were grimly accusatory. 'He didn't turn up this morning and I have a none-too-smart dispenser trying to cope with all the back work. I sent one of the assistants round to Ross's rooms to find out what had happened to him — thought he was ill — but it seems he's left town. Departed last night without so much as a hint to his landlady where he was going. That being so he's finished here.'

The superintendent exchanged a glance with Grant. 'A pity,' he said, sighing. 'I wanted to get into touch with him most urgently.'

'Concerning what?' Granwell asked curiously. 'First he disappears without warning, then the police want to interview him. Anything I can ask about?'

'Afraid not, sir,' Denning answered. 'You will have the address where he lived, of course? I'd be glad of it.'

'Er — yes.' Granwell rose and went to a filing cabinet. He searched through a card-index and then said; 'Fifteen Sunnydown Road. Mrs. Smith was his landlady. The road's just off Halingford Road as you go towards Werton.'

'I know it, sir, thanks,' Denning said, rising — and Grant jotted the address down in his notebook.

'Tell me something, Superintendent.' Granwell asked. 'Has your wanting to see Ross anything to do with that fishmonger's explosion down the road this morning?'

As Denning hesitated, Granwell continued: 'I've been reading about it in tonight's paper. Damned queer business. First a mystery note cut from newspaper headlines, then police protection, then the explosion — and that poor devil Bilkin killed. Naturally I'm not saying Ross had anything to do with it — I've respect for the law concerning slander.

But I certainly can't help putting two and two together. That Bilkin should ever have been killed at all seems a pretty sad reflection on the police.'

'We're not supermen, sir,' Denning said, now resolved to divulge no information whatever.

'I agree.' Granwell looked at Denning steadily. 'But I think you could have done better! It seems to me that there has been some deliberate negligence somewhere, a fact I shan't forget to mention at the next Council meeting. Better watch yourself, Superintendent. Inefficiency is something which can't be tolerated when it involves loss of life and property.'

'You can rest assured, sir, that I'm doing my best,' Denning answered, controlling his temper.

'I wish I could! Where does Ross fit in — or don't you want to say?'

'I'm not at liberty to do so, sir — sorry. Thanks for his address. I'll see if I can get in touch with him.'

With this Denning took his departure, Grant beside him. Coming to the outdoors they began walking back across the street towards the superintendent's official car outside the police station.

'Likeable sort of chap, sir,' Grant commented dryly.

'He behaved exactly as I expected,' Denning sighed. 'I've noticed his antics in the Council debates; the *Gazette* reporters have a passion for burlesquing him, and I'm not surprised. Anyway, be damned to him. Our worry is trying to find this chap Ross.'

'Going to his rooms now, sir?' Grant asked, as they stopped beside the car.

'Yes. Sooner we get in touch with him the better.'

Grant settled at the steering wheel and Denning into the seat beside him.

'Certainly,' Denning said, as the car got underway, 'the coincidence of Ross buying the 'message newspapers' and then doing a disappearing act is too obvious to miss. As head dispenser he must also be an able chemist. That might points perhaps to a chemical explanation for the explosion which destroyed Bilkin's shop.'

'When criminals start to use laboratory technique to gain their ends it makes the going tough . . . But how do we reconcile the fact that Ross left Halingford last night and yet the explosion occurred this morning?'

'We don't *know* that Ross left Halingford last night. He might not have gone until after the explosion — ingeniously prepared beforehand — and somehow got through the police watch. And,' Denning added grimly, 'if we are dealing with something chemical I agree with you that it's going to be a hard nut to crack. Neither of us are chemists.'

The vision of having to call on Scotland Yard clouded Denning's mind for a moment. Not if he could help it!

Presently they reached the unpretentious stucco-fronted house where Clayton Ross had had board-residence, and after a brief flurry of alarm at discovering two uniformed police officials on her doorstep, Mrs. Smith — a thin, elderly woman of surprising gentility — ushered them both into the living room and shut the front door quickly.

'This is a bit of a shock to me,' she gave a troubled smile. 'Finding the police on my doormat.'

'Sorry to upset you,' Denning apologized, 'but I won't take up too much of your time. I'm anxious to have an interview with Mr. Ross. I believe he had rooms here?'

'Until last night, yes. Then he paid me a week's money in lieu of notice and said he was leaving. He didn't say why, or where he was going. He simply packed his bags and went. I was sorry to lose him,' Mrs. Smith added almost sadly.

'How did he seem last night?' Denning questioned. 'Was he moody, in good spirits, or what?'

'He appeared worried, as if something was preying on his mind . . . What has he done, Inspector?' Mrs. Smith asked.

'I'm sorry, madam, but I can't tell you that. Do you happen to have any idea where he might have gone?'

'I'm afraid not,' she answered. 'He said very little about his private affairs. I think he took his work very seriously, though he was inclined to have what you might call 'revolutionary' tendencies. 'Up the workers' and all that kind of thing.'

Denning nodded understandingly. 'Did this 'revolutionary' tendency take any specific form?'

'Well, he was always telling my husband that his employer, Mr. Granwell, whom I suppose you know, was a slave driver. I gathered that he developed this belief from having to work in a basement dispensary where he felt cramped, imprisoned. He often spoke of asking Mr. Granwell to provide him with larger quarters. Whether he ever did ask him or not I don't know.'

'Evidently he had no love for Mr. Granwell, then,' Denning said, thoughtfully. 'Anything else you can tell me?'

'I don't think so. He had no parents living. In fact I think his only interest in life was a girl called Claire — his fiancée.'

'And where does she live?' Denning asked sharply. 'He may have got into touch with her.'

'There I can't help you,' Mrs. Smith said regretfully. 'He only spoke of her as Claire, but I never got her surname, or any address details.'

'Isn't it possible,' Grant said, looking up from making shorthand jottings in his notebook, 'that this girl Claire wrote Ross now and again? Didn't you ever see any letters from her to Ross, and perhaps remember the postmark?'

Mrs. Smith looked surprised. 'Why, yes. There was often a letter on a Monday morning, but the postmarks were always different. I don't think I ever saw two consecutive.'

'Evidently a girl who travels about,' Denning muttered. 'One thing more I'd like, and that's a description of Mr. Ross.'

'Oh, he's thin, about five feet nine, with fair hair and grey eyes. Usually he went about in a mackintosh and brown trilby hat. At least that is what he had on when he left me — and a navy blue suit.'

'Thanks,' Denning said, rising, 'You've been very kind, Mrs. Smith. Sorry we had to bother you.'

They returned to the police station, where Denning motioned the detective-sergeant to accompany him into his office.

'Ross,' Denning said resolutely, putting his uniform cap on the desk, 'has got to be found! He begins to look as though he had the devil of a lot to do with this game.'

'Yes, sir. I suppose the only thing we can do to begin with is circularize all other stations to keep an eye open for him.'

'I'll see to that all right,' Denning answered. 'In the meantime let's see how far we've got. Take a seat, Grant.'

Grant sat down and studied the notes he had made so far. 'It seems certain that it was this chap Ross who sent the warning,' he said. 'But it seems such a contradictory thing to do if he was the one who caused the explosion. That is, if he wanted to include the Bilkin family in the explosion. If he didn't, then presumably he sent it to get them out of the way. We can assume that he made it his business to watch if the Bilkins heeded his advice. They didn't, but he blew the place up just the same. And he got out of town before it blew up, perhaps to give himself an alibi by not even being in the district.'

'There is also another possibility,' Denning mused. 'If we are mixed up in a crime which concerns chemicals it may well be that whatever caused the explosion was already planted in the shop — skilfully concealed — and Ross jumped to the conclusion that the Bilkin family would leave the property. When they didn't it was impossible to retrieve the — whatever it was, because the place was guarded, so he got out of the district and the shop went sky high. I'm not suggesting that P.C. Saunders didn't search properly — but it's a difficult job to find a chemical set-up when you're looking for something resembling an infernal machine.'

'That's probably the most likely possibility of the lot,' Grant admitted. 'But what was his motive?'

'Let's consider the man's psychology for a moment,' Denning said. 'He has the brains to be a head dispenser — so may also have had the brains to blow that place up without leaving a trace. We know he was prone to 'isms': is he, let us say, a 'case', the sort of person who believes in slum clearance as the path to a better Britain? Believing in even that possibility he might have considered he was doing society a service by blowing up that old-fashioned shop. It was one of the oldest places in the town.'

'In other words, a dangerous crank?' Grant suggested.

'Why not? Such eccentrics don't behave like ordinary people, and sometimes they'll go to the most extraordinary lengths to prove their point.'

The superintendent was quite aware that he was stretching possibility to the limit — but it was a possibility, and at the moment the only one in the whole puzzling business.

'That girl friend of his — Claire somebody,' Grant mused. 'What do you imagine she can be to write from a different place every week?'

'At a guess, I'd say a variety artiste,' Denning replied. 'Or an actress. Better see what we can find out about her.'

'How? Claire Blank won't get us very far.'

'Most young men are proud enough of

being attached to a girl — and especially if she happens to be in the public eye — to mention the fact. I'll take a bet on it that Ross has mentioned her to somebody at the emporium, if only to the under-dispenser with whom he worked. We'll see what he has to say for himself and — '

Denning broke off as the sergeant-in-charge tapped on the door and entered. It was unnecessary for him to announce the visitor for it was the tall, genial person of Colonel Barrow, the Chief Constable for the county, who came in.

Everybody liked Colonel Barrow — his good nature was a byword. Sandy-haired, eagle-nosed, keen-eyed, he shook hands with both the superintendent and detective-sergeant as he greeted them.

'Thought I'd find you here even though it's past your usual time,' he explained, sitting down at the desk. 'I came as soon as I could after receiving your report, Denning . . . How are things going on with this nasty business of Bilkin?'

'Not half as well as I'd like, sir.' Denning grimaced. 'The two main stumbling blocks are lack of definite motive for the crime, and the means by which the crime was committed.'

'The motive and the means, eh? Well, since they are the fundamentals of any crime, you seem to be in a bad way! Let me have the details.'

Denning gave them.

'On the face of it,' Colonel Barrow said, 'it does look as though Ross might have something to do with it, though we have to guard between circumstantial and direct evidence. I don't place much faith in the newsagents having seen him buy a paper, except the one who knew Ross to be Granwell's chief dispenser. That lead is sound enough. Just the same Ross must be interviewed and account for his movements. Until you can catch up with him what else do you propose doing?'

'I had thought of interviewing the assistant dispenser with whom Ross worked and seeing if he happens to know anything about Claire, this girlfriend of Ross's. When in trouble, a man usually flies to a woman. So where she is, he may be also.'

'Well, it's good psychology, but consider the practical standpoint first. It's more than possible that this assistant dispenser is a friend of Ross's, especially if there be only two of them. There is nothing to prevent him giving the tip-off to Ross — if he knows where he is — that we're after him . . . In other words, I don't think we should betray our hands too much. If Ross is as important as we think he is, we've got to get him — and we'll never do it if we herald our coming with a fanfare of trumpets.'

'Yes, sir, I see your point,' Denning agreed, though privately he did not agree in the least.

'I think that circularizing the other stations is the best move,' the Colonel added, thinking.

'But you do agree it is possible Ross may be with this girl, sir? I remain pretty sanguine that if we can locate her we can almost locate him.'

'Yes, but the possibility is that she is a variety artiste. 'Claire' may not be the stage name she uses, so it would be useless to try tracing it. She might only be in a chorus, in which case her name would never even appear on the bills.' The Chief Constable shook his sandy head. 'Be too much valuable time wasted there, Denning. It's only worth a try as a last resort. Do your utmost to trace Ross through the usual channels and make your next duty that of getting the report of the insurance company's fire assessor.'

'I had thought of doing that in any case, sir,' Denning replied. 'Even though I have Brewster's opinions I'm not entirely satisfied — '

'He can't be compared with an expert assessor from an insurance company,' the Chief Constable said decisively. 'Those men never miss the vaguest hint of a clue. See what he has to say and then decide your course of action from his report. He should be here in the morning, shouldn't he?'

'I'll be surprised if he isn't,' Denning answered dryly.

Pause, as Colonel Barrow speculated further. 'Chemical plot, eh? In the case of Ross I admit his position as dispenser would give him a tremendous advantage.

Suppose it is a chemical crime? Do you think you can handle it?'

'I'm no chemist, sir, but I believe in finishing anything I start. One thing I don't intend to do and that is make it necessary for the Yard to help us.'

'Commendable, of course — and dammit, I've full faith in you and the detective-sergeant here — but we've other people to please. The Yard is the only body able to call on the necessary experts to sort out a chemical problem.'

'I'd rather like to handle this in my own way, sir, if I may,' Denning said, after a pause. 'I'll keep you in touch with all I do, and if in the end you don't think I'm making progress, it'll be up to you to give me further instructions.'

This apparently was good enough for the Chief Constable. He left the police station perfectly satisfied that all that could be done by the ambitious superintendent would be done. What he did not know was that, in spite of himself, Denning kept thinking about a little man who looked like the traditional bust of Beethoven.

9

With all police departments circularized to be on the look-out for Clayton Ross, Denning thankfully ended his day's work. He was back at his office in the police station bright and early the following morning and had not been at his desk above five minutes before the relieved constable from the Bilkin site came to make his report.

He went through the routine details with a stolid regard for officialdom, concluding: ' . . . and so there's nothing unusual to report, sir. I didn't let a single thing slip by me.'

'I'm sure you didn't,' Denning agreed. 'And Benson has now taken over?'

'That's right, sir. He now has the instructions that you gave me. If anybody turns up to assess the damage they're to report to you afterwards.'

Denning nodded and the constable left the office.

For some while after this the superintendent was busy with Grant, checking over the previous day's notes and, between them, studying the morning papers for any chance word or hint that might possibly point to the whereabouts of Clayton Ross.

They failed to discover anything, but it was noteworthy that the mystery of the Halingford fire had penetrated as far as the daily papers and was being discussed at some length by the crime reporters.

Those with a scientific bent detailed complicated formulae guaranteed to produce a fire; others were more interesting and recalled famous fire-raisers of the past and the particular methods they had adopted. In none of them, however, was there any clue as to how the Halingford business had been accomplished. The general effect produced on Denning was one of exasperation.

'I thought this would happen,' he snapped, throwing the paper down. 'If Bilkin hadn't shown that warning to his friends we might have kept it quiet — but our local newshounds got the information, passed it on, and there we are.'

Denning let the matter drop. Back of his mind he knew he was only killing time, waiting for the insurance fire assessor to come on the scene and say his piece — which at eleven o'clock he did.

Montague Vincent was fat and broad-shouldered, in a raglan mackintosh, and with ginger hair sprouting rather after the fashion of coconut-bristles on top of an egg-shaped head. He presented himself in Denning's office and declared without blinking an eyelid that his company would not pay as much as a penny.

'Because you've found something which proves it to be a deliberate case of arson?' Denning asked.

'I haven't found anything,' Montague Vincent replied calmly. 'I simply came to examine the business as a matter of routine. What kills the claim is the fact that it is now known almost throughout the country that Mr. Bilkin was warned beforehand. That in itself is sufficient to preclude all possibility of an accident.

The explosion must have been *contrived* . . . somehow.'

'It's not my job to argue this insurance claim, of course,' the superintendent said. 'You'll do that with Mrs. Bilkin's own assessor, but I am interested in the mechanics. You are perfectly sure there is no trace of anything in that debris which might prove it was an explosion deliberately caused?'

'Perfectly sure,' the fire assessor answered flatly. 'I have examined the remains of fires for the past twenty years and never made a mistake.'

'That being so,' Denning said, 'Mrs. Bilkin might stand a chance of getting her money. That warning to the Bilkin family to get out did not specify *what* danger, and since the place blew up afterwards it was assumed that that had been the danger referred to. If you cannot find a single shred of evidence to prove the explosion was deliberately arranged your company might have to pay up after all.'

'I shall contest the claim to the last ditch! I would say that without a completely comprehensive policy Mrs.

Bilkin will not stand much chance. Not that the company is hard-hearted, of course, but naturally it is businesslike.'

'All right, it isn't my province,' Denning sighed. 'Thanks, Mr. Vincent. I'm sorry you couldn't be of more help to me.'

The fire assessor shrugged and took his departure. Grant, who had been seated in silence listening to the conversation, looked at his superior enquiringly.

'That scotches that, sir!'

'Afraid so,' Denning admitted, rubbing his chin. 'Whether Mrs. Bilkin gets that badly needed money or not now depends a great deal on police findings — on proving whether or not that warning note applied to the explosion or something totally different. What we have to do is find out how that confounded explosion was *caused* — whether it was an Act of God or ingeniously prepared. To cut it short I think I've got to eat humble pie and pay a call on Dr. Carruthers.'

'The trouble is.' Grant muttered morosely, 'he's such a cocky little devil. Once he gets started he may take the thing right out of our hands.'

'Not if I can help it,' Denning declared. 'Besides, he did tell me that he hasn't the slightest interest in police procedure — that his only reason for helping in such cases is to get to the root of the scientific implications. The point is this, Grant — if I don't get outside aid from an expert in chemistry and kindred subjects I'll never get anywhere. That will mean the Yard, and what glory — and possible promotion — I might have squeezed out of solving this problem will dissipate . . . '

Denning got to his feet decisively. 'Come with me and we'll see what sort of a mood our pint-sized friend is in.'

Dr. Carruthers was in quite a good mood: there was nothing more certain to make him purr than to let him believe he had suddenly become indispensable; this apart from his natural interest in a scientific problem.

The moment he realized the nature of the superintendent's visit, he put aside the work he had been doing with Gordon Drew and gave his entire attention to the superintendent's story.

Denning did not keep back a single detail. There was an unexpected relief in being able to plant the whole thing piecemeal in the lap of a man who had many times contributed surprising and deadly accurate sidelights on off-the-track problems.

'So, Doctor,' he finished quietly, 'it seems to me that you being a chemist, a physicist, and a man whose knowledge the police call upon some-times, I thought you might have some ideas — '

'Yes, that's possible,' Carruthers conceded dryly. 'And it's no surprise you've come to me: I've been expecting it. I don't think you are up against an ordinary crook by any means. There's a subtlety about this damned business which appeals to me.'

'I'm doing this off my own bat,' Denning admitted. 'The Chief Constable doesn't know anything about it.'

'Not yet,' Carruthers murmured. 'Colonel Barrow is a very good personal friend of mine. Grand fellow — but a rotten chess player.'

Getting up he poured himself half a cup of tea, drank it while he pondered. Then he gave an elfish grin. 'You've got yourself in one deuce of a mess son haven't you?'

Though the reference to 'son' stung him slightly Denning gave a grudging nod and a smile. 'When we get an explosion which has no apparent cause I hold up my hands.'

'Explosions just don't happen for the fun of it,' Carruthers remarked. 'There are a dozen possible causes for them, but from what you've told me so far, I haven't the vaguest idea how it was done.'

'Oh,' Denning said, clearly disappointed.

'Hang it all, boy, you don't expect anything from those details, do you? The only persons who called at the shop on the morning of the disaster were the policeman on duty and the ice-man, who was new to the game and didn't know his job. He delivered ice of a yellowish colour and went to the extraordinary length of wrapping felt round it instead of using the ice-tongs as an experienced man would have done. Then what? He delivered his charge with the care of a mother putting an infant to bed. Presumably he behaved like that because he wasn't used to throwing ice blocks about. If there was a deeper meaning to it I'll have to think a good deal before I find it. You have yourself thought of one possibility — an infernal machine in the ice, and since you are satisfied that that is out who am I to question it?'

'I thought you might like to examine the debris for possible traces of the explosion's cause?' Denning suggested, with a hint of desperation.

'When the fire chief and two insurance assessors have already done it? Not I! I'd merely waste valuable time. At the moment,' Carruthers went on, 'the thing which intrigues me most is the surprising care exercised by the lorry man in delivering the ice. Such care is not exactly a highly developed virtue in a truck driver. I must think that over as I continue with my work, and some sort of idea might form. Until then . . . '

Carruthers broke off at a tap on the

door and the dour-faced housekeeper came in.

'There's a Mr. Granwell here, Doctor. Says he wants to see Superintendent Denning right away.'

Denning's eyes brightened. 'Maybe he has some news concerning Ross.'

'Have him come in, please,' the scientist instructed.

When he did arrive the emporium owner's normally pink face was red, either from exertion or emotion, and there was alarm peering out of his grey-blue eyes. His mat of woolly brown hair looked as though he had not stopped to brush it.

Without so much as a word of greeting to any of the assembled men he pushed a cheap envelope into the surprised Denning's hand.

'Read that!' he commanded. '*Read* it!'

Denning pulled the cheap slip of notepaper out of the envelope, even though he knew what was coming, for the address was arranged in letters cut from a newspaper. The message itself, word for word was identical to the one Oscar

Bilkin had received:

GET OUT BEFORE TOMORROW.
YOU ARE ALL IN DANGER

Silence. Denning's face showed he was struggling to control his feelings. Carruthers took the note and read it aloud. Then he looked at the envelope.

'Posted in Halingford last night, Wednesday,' he commented. 'Hmmm . . .'

Now the immediate sensation was over Rupert Granwell took upon himself to explain. 'It came by this morning's mail, Superintendent. I found it on my desk with the rest of my letters — '

'On your desk, sir? I presume that the letters are sorted by a clerk before being passed to the various departments?'

'Naturally. There are two girls who attend to incoming and outgoing mail. Why?'

'I was just thinking,' Denning said. 'The girl who first saw the letter must have known — if she reads the papers — that an address done in this fashion could only imply another warning. That's a pity. It destroys the chance of keeping the thing quiet. However, go on. When you found the letter what did you do?'

'I dashed out to the police station with it straight away and was told you had gone out. Fortunately, my position in this town — councillor, you know — made that obtuse young sergeant-in-charge divulge your whereabouts. Well, what are you going to do? Let my emporium be blown to bits, just as Bilkin's was?'

'Of course not!' Denning replied curtly. 'This time we know that the thing isn't a joke. We'll examine that emporium of yours from top to bottom — '

'You did that with Bilkin's,' Granwell interrupted. 'And look what happened!'

'That job was undertaken by a constable,' Denning said. 'He's a good man, but not a superman. He may have missed something. I'll do the job myself this time, with Detective-Sergeant Grant here to help me. After that I'll have the place surrounded with all the available men I can get. You for your part, Mr. Granwell, had better have your staff cease work at dinner time and — '

'They will in any case. Thursday is half closing day in Halingford, remember.'

'All the better,' Denning nodded; he had overlooked the fact. 'From noon onwards, then, we'll take charge.'

'Whatever you say,' Granwell assented. 'It seems pretty clear to me now that we have that crazy ex-dispenser of mine, Clayton Ross, to deal with. Why he blew up Bilkin's place I don't know, unless it was for experimental purposes. But I can guess why he wants to wreck my place — because he considered himself badly treated in the basement dispensary. I never did trust him very much. He has quite a lot of queer ideas that don't belong in business. You've *got* to find him, Superintendent!'

'Suppose you just leave things with me, sir?' Denning suggested quietly.

'Well — all right.' Granwell turned to go. 'I'll get back to the emporium. When I've closed down should I come to the police station and advise you?'

'If you will,' Denning said.

Evidently too worried to consider formalities Granwell left without a handshake.

'If I fail this time to prevent a disaster

I'm liable to go back to pounding a beat,' Denning muttered. 'Granwell has influence with the Council and the Chief Constable. My trouble is that even when I go to the emporium I shall not know what to look for. I'll be little better than Saunders was.'

'After all this effort, son, I can't just stand by and see you take a nose dive,' Carruthers said. 'I'll come with you and have a look at the place.'

'I'd be grateful if you would, sir,' Denning said, and he meant it. He was reasonably sure that nothing of a chemical or explosive nature, would escape the eye of an expert physicist.

'I suppose you'll want this message for analysis?' Carruthers said, handing it back

'Definitely,' Denning assented. 'The other one was made from cuttings out of seven different newspapers. This one looks as though every cutting has come from one newspaper.' He studied it intently. 'However, I must get a proper report. You'd better get off to Werton with it right away, Grant.'

'Why?' Carruthers asked calmly. 'What

do you think I have a laboratory in the basement for? Let me have it: I'll tell you everything you need to know within a few minutes.' And with a confident look he went from the Den.

Gordon Drew busied himself with tidying up the work the scientist and he had been engaged upon. Then presently Carruthers came back and handed the note and envelope over to the superintendent.

'All from one newspaper,' he announced. 'And from the pink tint it has I'd suggest the *Halingford Gazette*. Their newsprint has that particularly distinctive hue.'

'I wonder which issue it was?' Denning mused.

'Last night's,' Carruthers said, and at Denning's enquiring look, he added: 'If you'll notice, one of those capital 'A's' has a broken crosspiece. Only slight, but it's there. I noticed it in a headline in the *Gazette* last night. Naturally the fault would repeat throughout the entire edition. It's last night's all right.'

'And this paper can only be bought in Halingford!' Denning exclaimed. 'That means that Ross must have had the nerve to go out and buy it — and none of the men I have watching saw him. Probably a street-vendor,' he decided. 'Just the same, Grant, you might go round the news-agents again and see what you can find. Maybe Ross hasn't left the district after all, and is lying low somewhere.'

Grant nodded and left to commence his mission. Carruthers led the way into the hall, donned his overcoat, and jammed his black homberg on his head; then when Gordon Drew had got into his topcoat Denning led the way out to the car.

In ten minutes they had reached the police station and here they remained until five past one, discussing all aspects of the matter.

Finally Rupert Granwell arrived and announced that the emporium was empty of staff and customers from basement to top floor. This fact took Denning, Carruthers, and Gordon Drew across the road in a matter of minutes, Granwell following behind them with an obvious air of reluctance.

'Afraid you'll be blown up?' Carruthers

asked cynically, as the emporium owner fiddled with a bunch of keys before the massive main doors of the place.

Granwell glared. 'Of course I'm afraid! I haven't forgotten the way Bilkin got the works. Nothing to stop it happening here at any moment, is there?'

'The time limit mentioned in the warning has not yet expired,' Carruthers answered. 'It said get out before tomorrow, remember. That, technically, means anything can happen after midnight tonight. Until then I should imagine you're safe enough.'

Granwell merely grunted; then he got the doors open at last.

Denning, Carruthers, and Gordon Drew followed him into the main ground floor department, and after departing to a switch-room Granwell snapped every light into being, ensuring that every hole and corner was brightly illuminated.

'You look for the obvious things, Superintendent,' Carruthers said. 'Gordon and I will scout round for the unexpected. This job is likely to take at least three hours.'

It took them nearly four, Granwell 'phoning a café around two o'clock and telling them to send in lunch.

During the lunch he was jumpy and ate little, and the rest of the time he either followed Carruthers and Gordon Drew, or the superintendent, as they went on their various peregrinations. Altogether it meant examining three departmental floors.

The ground floor contained chiefly clothing, drapery, and haberdashery.

On shelves and stands, models and racks, there were countless numbers of clothes, oblong rolls of cloth, some of it woollen and some of it flimsy and inflammable. In fact the entire ground floor — as Carruthers pointed out — was a fire-raiser's paradise *if* fire was to be the crime aimed at.

The second floor, devoted to furniture, was just as dangerous a proposition, everything being wood or upholstery; whereas the third floor was more or less a general miscellany of all kinds — about fifty per cent metalwork.

So to the offices, including Granwell's

own, but there was nothing here beyond normal office furniture, and steel filing cabinets.

An hour having been devoted by all the party to each department they returned to the ground floor and looked at Carruthers expectantly.

'So far, nothing wrong,' he announced. I haven't spotted anything suggestive of an infernal machine or gadget for fire-raising nor have I seen anything of a prepared chemical nature that after a time might cause heat through combustion. There are plenty of chemicals and byproducts that can do that, but I'm not going through the list. I will mention one angle that occurred to me though — namely, some of these drapery goods might have been nitrated beforehand and returned to stock. The fact of them having been thus treated would not normally be visible — except to the practiced eye — but one spark on them and — whoof!' Carruthers spread his hands expressively.

'Oh?' Granwell looked interested but vague. 'I'm afraid I don't understand. I'm no chemist. I leave that to the dispensing department.'

'It's simple enough,' Carruthers said, seeming impatient that he should have to explain. 'Nitrates are combinations of nitric acid with various bases — such as nitrate of barium, nitrate of calcium, nitrate of copper, and so on. They are soluble in water and it is possible to treat cloth, especially the lighter kinds you have here, with it. It then becomes, for all practical purposes, gun-cotton. A spark, even the merest touch of a lighted cigarette, would be sufficient to explode the nitrate and the material so treated.

'If several of these dress lengths and draperies here were so treated your emporium would go up like a torch at a mere spark. Only there's nothing wrong. Everything is normal. I was, you see, considering the possibility that Ross, as a chemist, might have planned the idea long beforehand and spent some time — maybe at night — in the laboratory treating different materials in readiness. You'd never know of it.'

'What if he had done that and some of

the treated lengths had been sold to customers?'

'I imagine he would only treat the stuff which was not intended for customers — those window hangings, those traveller's sample lengths for exhibition only, and so on . . . But, anyway I'm wrong. This place is normal enough, though it would burn like Hades in midsummer if it did catch fire. I think we'd better take a look at the dispensary and see what we can find there.'

'Good idea,' Granwell agreed, and led the way to the service lift. It took the quartet down into the brightly lighted area of bottles and chemical impedimenta about which Clayton Ross had had such disparaging remarks to make.

As they entered the dispensary the men stood looking musingly about them.

'And Ross complained because these quarters were not good enough,' Gordon Drew commented. 'They look all right to me. That was what he said, Super, wasn't it?'

'So his landlady told me, yes.'

'It's right enough,' Granwell confirmed.

'As I understand it, he was going to come and 'lay his case' before me, but for some reason never did. According to Jones, the assistant dispenser, Ross left the dispensary here to come to my office, was away for a few minutes, and then returned — his mission unfulfilled.'

'When did this happen?' Denning asked sharply. 'I don't recall you mentioning it before, sir.'

'Too damned trivial! It was on Monday. He was going to speak to me at five-thirty when he thought he'd catch me alone, but evidently he must have changed his mind.'

Denning brooded over this revelation in silence, making no attempt to assist Carruthers in an examination of the dispensary. Here, the Superintendent realized, he was out of his depth. But it gave him a chance to think about what Granwell had said.

Denning resolved to have an early word with the assistant dispenser. He perhaps was the one person who could fit the missing parts into the puzzle of Clayton Ross.

'Nothing either in here or in these adjoining stockrooms which has any special significance,' Carruthers said, after he had completed his search with Gordon Drew at his side. 'I feel I should mention though that there is a source of danger in those drums of paraffin in the adjoining stockroom there — '

'But they're sealed,' Granwell pointed out. 'We have to store them, after all. Quite a number of customers want paraffin.'

'Yes,' Carruthers admitted, 'I suppose so. As to these shelves,' he went on, surveying the dispensary as a whole, 'there are several substances which are harmless enough in themselves but highly dangerous in combination — ammonia, hydro-chloric acid, glycerine, mercury . . . Yes indeed! However, with all the stoppers on and none of these various things in combination with each other I'm willing to stake my reputation on the fact that there is no reason to fear either explosion or fire in this whole place.'

'Thank heaven for that!' Granwell said in relief.

'I suppose this place will be covered by insurance, sir?' Denning asked.

Granwell nodded briefly. 'You suppose right, Superintendent. With the Allied and Industrial Insurance Trust. What kind of a businessman do you think I am? It's fully covered for the highest amount I could get. Not a question of premiums, either: I would have had the amount twice as much only the company wouldn't indemnify me any higher because of the inflammable nature of my stock. So even if it did come to them paying out, it would still be a pretty poor recompense for the business I have here.'

The superintendent nodded but did not pursue the matter further. He had asked the question more as a point of routine than anything else, to determine if it might be worthwhile to ingeniously destroy the place. Certainly it might — but evidently the place had more value as it stood. And would any insurance company in its right senses pay out on the claim if warning of the disaster were known to have been sent beforehand?

'That seems to be all, then,' Carruthers

said. 'The rest is up to you, Superintendent. I've done all I can.'

'Yes, I'll — ' Denning paused, his attention caught suddenly by something. It was the top of a newspaper — on which were the words — ETTE — sticking out of the metal wastebasket under the bench. Stooping, he pulled the newspaper out and flattened its crumpled pages on the bench. The others looked on interestedly. From the centre pages captions had been neatly cut out.

10

'It's last night's *Halingford Gazette*,' Granwell said at last, with a grim glance at Carruthers. 'And from the look of it the one from which my warning note was pieced together.'

Denning pulled the note from his pocket and opened it out. It only took a few moments to check the fact that this was the identical paper from which the lettering had been extracted.

'Have you a night watchman on these premises, Mr. Granwell?' Denning asked, returning the note to his wallet.

'Well, yes . . . ' Granwell spoke slowly. 'I hesitate because he's not half so efficient as he might be. But at the moment he's the best I can find. He's getting old and rather slow. Why do you ask?'

'It seems that Ross came back in here last night, presumably after the staff had left, and pieced together that message to you. Then he threw the paper in the bin here . . . ' Denning reflected, obviously not satisfied. 'It would have been far more prudent to burn the paper. Wonder if Jones noticed it? Still, even if he did he would have no reason to attach special significance to it . . . '

'Perhaps,' Granwell said, 'he was too busy, anyway.'

Dr. Carruthers mused, looking like a composer meditating over a symphony as he stared at the newspaper. He gave a slight start when Denning drew it gently from beneath his gaze preparatory to putting it in his pocket.

'How would Ross get into the building?' Gordon asked. 'Has he a pass-key?'

'No,' Granwell answered. 'I'm the only one with keys — that is, excepting the general manager and night watchman, and neither of them would allow their keys to leave their possession.'

'Which makes it seem impossible that Ross, once out of the building, could ever get into it again,' Denning commented.

'There might be a way, through an upper window maybe,' Granwell answered. 'Ross began with us when we opened, two years ago, and has had ample opportunity to discover all the ins and outs. Certainly he'd know how to circumvent the watchman — and in moving from one department to another the stock would afford concealment.'

Denning shrugged. 'Well, I'll leave that part to fit itself in later. Within the next hour, Mr. Granwell, I'll have six men guarding this place from the outside — and I'll see to it that six men, relieving each other, keep their eyes on this place until midnight tomorrow night. I'll have to borrow reinforcements from Werton, but it will be done.'

'I think,' Carruthers remarked, 'we might go even further than that. The best opportunity for dirty work will be by night. I think that we — that is you, Superintendent, the sergeant, Gordon, and myself — should also watch this place throughout the night hours. We shall lose our beauty sleep and probably get frozen stiff, but we can hardly hope to get to the bottom of this problem without some inconvenience.'

Denning did not even hesitate. 'I was going to do that with the sergeant in any case, but naturally I hadn't intended to suggest that you do it too . . . '

'Well, I'm going to, so say no more about it. So — at six o'clock tonight when it gets dark we begin our vigil.'

'Naturally,' Granwell said, 'I shall join you. It's my place and I think it's only right that I should. I'll also take care to fix it up with Hunter at the teashop that he serves refreshment to us at intervals during the night. I can manage it . . . being a councillor.'

'The more the merrier,' Carruthers remarked. 'I suggest we all meet at the police station at six o'clock — your men, Denning, to start on guard an hour hence.'

So it was agreed and they returned upstairs to the ground floor.

'Six o'clock, then,' Granwell said, seeing them to the front door. 'I've some correspondence to finish and I might as well get it done. I feel safe in doing it now you've been over the place: I had the wind up before. I'll join you later, gentlemen, and anybody who can get through a guard like that will be a magician indeed!'

Upon returning to the police station across the road Denning found that Grant had returned from his tour of the newsagents with the somewhat sobering report that nobody even resembling Clayton Ross could be recalled by any of the newsagents.

Either Ross had never bought a paper, or more likely, none of the newsagents could really remember. As Denning well knew, this was a weak line of enquiry, even though it had to be followed on the off chance that it might yield something.

'Well, that's that,' Denning said, when he had had the news. 'We've checked up on the emporium and found it okay, but I also found the newspaper from which, apparently, the warning note to Granwell was made . . . '

He explained the details, and added; 'I'm going on to Dr. Carruthers' place. He's in the car waiting for me. He says he'll make all the analysis necessary from this paper and so keep Werton out of it.

You'd better stay here in case anything important breaks, and also fix the detailing of the men to guard the emporium . . . '

He gave the detective-sergeant the necessary instructions and then returned to his car where, seated in the back, the physicist and Gordon Drew were waiting for him.

Immediately they had returned to Carruthers' home the little scientist threw aside his homberg and overcoat and led the way down the stairs into his well-equipped laboratory.

Denning and Gordon Drew looked on as he got busy with a binocular-microscope upon both the newspaper and the note itself. Altogether he was about half an hour on the job and then handed both the note and newspaper back to Denning.

'The note definitely came from that,' he said. 'In some instances the cutting edge of letter and newspaper match in every particular. The letters were cut out with a pair of slightly curved nail-scissors. You might want to bear that in mind.'

'I shall,' Denning agreed. 'And thanks for your help.'

Carruthers grinned, 'Don't mention it; I'm enjoying myself . . . But look here, do you really believe that any man would be such a blasted fool as to push the newspaper he'd used in a bin for everybody to find?'

'No,' Denning admitted. 'Even less do I trust the way it was pushed in, with the last half of the word 'Gazette' showing. I think it's a plant . . . ' He frowned. 'I'm convinced that Ross is responsible, otherwise why did he disappear so promptly? Yet if this newspaper was a plant it suggests that Ross did not send the second warning. Added to that is the fact that I can't trace him having bought a local paper last night. So that leaves only one possibility — '

'And that is?'

'The assistant dispenser, Jones, must be interviewed. He too is a chemist, don't forget — and I can't quite understand him overlooking the *Gazette* in the bin. He could have put that paper in the bin just as easily as Ross.'

Carruthers nodded. 'Yes, true enough. Particularly as your suspicions regarding Ross seem to be abating.' At Denning's surprised look he added: 'I believe that you found it intriguing that Ross went upstairs to have it out with Granwell over his cramped quarters, and then didn't do it. Right? I was watching your face.'

'I'm left wondering why Ross didn't go through with his intention. I have the strangest feeling that his failure to carry out his plan may have some bearing on the problem. Only something most unusual could have stopped him, and that is what I find absorbing. Also,' Denning added, 'there's something else sticking in my mind concerning that *Gazette*, but I can't quite think what it is — yet.'

'If Ross,' Gordon Drew remarked, 'is not the one who sent the note to Granwell, who is? Outside Jones, I mean. And what is the motive?'

'That,' Denning said, 'is as foggy as the motive for blowing up Bilkin's place.'

'Another thing I don't understand,' Gordon went on, 'is the purpose of sending a warning beforehand.'

'Maybe it was intended to give even the night watchman a chance to get clear,' Denning responded, 'In that respect it worked because he won't be allowed in the building tonight.'

'There is also the other view,' Carruthers said, 'namely that a complete outsider, aware of what is going to happen, keeps sending the warnings in an effort to help the law but keep himself out of it. Or had you considered that?'

'Yes, sir, I had.' Denning remembered it had been one of his early theories. Then he glanced at his watch. 'I haven't got time now to call on this chap Jones — and I haven't got his address either. I'll get it from Granwell later and have Grant go over this evening and interview him while we keep our vigil. We've just time to have some tea and then get ready for action.'

'We'll have tea here,' Carruthers decided. 'There's some slab fruitcake on the agenda and I'm not missing that for all the vigils in the world. Lead the way upstairs, son, and I'll tell my housekeeper to hurry things up a bit.'

Their meal disposed of, the trio arrived at the police station again at ten to six, Denning going inside while Carruthers and Gordon Drew remained in the car. The sergeant was in the main enquiry office and Grant in his own sanctum, to which Denning went immediately.

Grant had, it appeared, detailed the necessary men to the emporium and all of them — with relief men arranged to take over at given times — were ensconced where they could watch and not be watched. The knowledge made Denning feel that he had taken every reasonable precaution that the law allowed.

'Granwell will be here at six,' he told Grant. 'I'm getting the address of that under-dispenser from him. I'll want you to go to his place and interview him. Get to know everything you can — tactfully. In particular try and find out if he noticed that *Gazette* in the bin, and if he has any idea why Ross didn't finish the job of seeing Granwell.'

'You can rely on me, sir,' Grant promised, and content with this assurance Denning gave his attention to a few routine matters until on the stroke of six Granwell arrived. He was muffled in a heavy overcoat, fur gloves, scarf, and golfing cap.

'All ready, I see,' he remarked, as he was shown into the detective-sergeant's office. 'I noticed Dr. Carruthers and that young chap are in the car. I've fixed up for refreshment to be brought to us outside the emporium at intervals.'

'Which will help a lot, sir,' Denning approved. 'Before we go, do you know the address of that under-dispenser of yours? Jones?'

'Jones?' Granwell repeated, surprised. 'Well, I can't tell it you offhand. It's in my files, of course. Does it matter?'

'Quite a lot. I wish to interview him.'

'I'm afraid it will have to wait. I'm not going back into the emporium for anybody — least of all for Jones address. Not now it's dark.'

'All right,' Denning shrugged, hiding his annoyance. 'I'll leave it until the morning.'

Granwell looked relived. He turned and led the way outside with Denning and Grant following him.

The only thing in their favour for the nocturnal vigil was that the weather had turned milder. Carruthers and Gordon Drew climbed out from the back of the police car to the pavement as the two came out of the police station.

In a little group the men crossed the road and Denning made it his first job to get a report of events to date. Nobody had entered the building, and the only person to leave it had been Granwell himself when he had finished attending to his correspondence.

Satisfied, Denning arranged the disposition of his men so that he and his own party could remain intact. Their vantage point was the big double doorway of a provision merchant's on the opposite corner to the emporium, a building where the windows had escaped the blast from the destroyed fish-shop.

'We can make this our base, without drawing attention to ourselves,' Denning explained, 'and perambulate from here as we see fit. I also have the fire brigade at the alert.'

'Which doesn't do us much good,' Granwell complained. 'If anything should happen wouldn't it be better to have it right outside the building in readiness?'

'And what do you suppose our criminal friend would do, sir, if he saw the fire brigade waiting?' Denning demanded.

'Scare him off, I expect. My property would at least be safer . . . All right,' Granwell growled. 'I'm taking the selfish viewpoint but you can't blame me for that. I have far more regard for the safety of my emporium than in seeing a damned criminal apprehended when it may be too late — as far as the emporium is concerned.'

'I know what I'm doing, sir,' Denning said quietly.

So the vigil began. At intervals Denning or Grant went on a tour of the concealed policemen and obtained their reports — which were negative; then at other periods one or other of the group would retire to the police station for a rest and a warm-up. The refreshment Granwell had ordered was duly brought towards ten o'clock.

The clock in the tower of St. Anne's struck midnight over a deserted Haling-ford and, perambulations at an end for the moment with the original group all gathered in the provision merchant's doorway, they prepared for more hours of weary waiting.

Then something happened! Gordon Drew saw it first and gripped the arm of Dr. Carruthers beside him. 'Look, sir! What's that?'

The group had all seen it at once. It was a yellow flicker of light that illuminated the windows of the ground floor department fronting to the right-angled street.

'Something or somebody!' Denning exclaimed. 'Come on! 'And have your key ready, sir,' he threw back at Granwell. Then he dived across the road.

A blast on Denning's whistle brought the hidden constables hurrying to his side while Granwell fumbled with the key to the double front doors. He turned it quickly in the lock and flung the doors wide — and on to an area which had become a blazing, tumbling confusion of flame and smoke.

Heat hurled itself at the men as they half entered the doorway. They had a vision of towers of crackling flame, of clothes and fabrics disintegrating in blazing sparks.

Flames were already sweeping in avid brilliance up the ornamental pillars supporting the ceiling. The banisters of the staircase leading to the upper floors were merely dark outlines against a hissing, spitting glare. Within minutes, it appeared, the entire ground floor had become an inferno.

'Get the fire brigade!' Denning ordered over his shoulder.

A constable dived for the fire-alarm box and Denning looked about him helplessly. Fire was flashing and spreading with inconceivable speed; there was also a smell of fumes . . . and they smelled of paraffin. The glare of the holocaust was already lighting the dark of the town and sending sparks and flame-painted spires of smoke upwards.

'How did it *happen*?' Granwell kept demanding, nearly dancing with futile rage.

Denning did not answer because he simply could not. Forced back to the other side of the street he stood with Carruthers, Gordon Drew, the detective-sergeant, and Granwell, staring at the devouring hell. The policemen had their hands full in other directions. Already, despite the hour, the inhabitants of Halingford were turning out to behold this latest display in pyrotechnics.

Then came the fire brigade, making the night hideous with its bell. A second engine came, and a third.

After half an hour's hopeless battle with the flames Werton had to supply three more auxiliaries. The main street became a wilderness of rubber hoses and slopping water. Foam extinguishers were also used without any appreciable effect.

Halingford was lighted from end to end with the most impressive fire it had ever had in its history.

Regardless of passing hours, of the smoke that made their eyes smart, the group on the other side of the street remained watching, scarcely commenting. To Denning, after all his precautions, it seemed impossible that such a disaster could have happened . . . But it had — and it was half past four before there remained only the blackened shell of the emporium and, within it, towering piles of darkly glowing ashes and debris.

'Apparently,' Carruthers said, arousing himself, 'that seems to be that!'

'We'd better get back to the police station and decide what comes next,' Denning said bitterly.

He turned to the nearest policeman, left orders that nobody was to go near the gutted building, and then picked his way through the pools of water and twisting hoses in pursuit of the four men going ahead of him down Halingford Road.

11

It was five o'clock in the morning. As they sat in the superintendent's office at the police station, thankful for chairs and the warmth of the fire, Denning's party kept glancing at each other sharply, waiting for the explosion of tempers, accusations, or — remote possibility — helpful suggestions.

The only one who seemed lost in speculations was Dr. Carruthers.

'I just don't understand it! We seem to be up against a pyromaniac with a gift for magic!' Denning declared at last.

'That,' Granwell pointed out sourly, 'is a damned silly remark from a superintendent of police! Pyromania may certainly enter into it, but not magic! We're up against somebody, or an organization, with more than their share of cunning. I've lost my entire business, and it's anybody's guess whether I'll ever get the insurance money. Which reminds me,'

Granwell broke off, 'do you mind if I use your 'phone, Super?'

Denning waved a hand and sat scowling in thought. Granwell spent a few minutes speaking to Amos Ballam, the local fire assessor, and gave him the details. The hour did not signify. Like all fire assessors, Amos Ballam was prepared to jump out of bed in the middle of the night and race post haste to any conflagration.

He promised to make an immediate thorough examination at dawn, by which time the ashes would have cooled somewhat and he would have light by which to investigate.

'I'll notify the insurance company first thing in the morning,' Granwell said, hanging up. 'Won't be anybody there at this time.'

'Well,' Granwell demanded, 'what are you going to do next, Superintendent? When do we start to get some action?'

'When I get a reasonable lead to follow up,' Denning answered sharply. 'All I can suggest is that somebody must have been concealed somewhere in the building and arranged the fire after we had all left and locked the place up. He could then perhaps have escaped through a window.'

'With our men watching all angles, sir?' Grant put in dubiously.

'Besides,' Granwell said, 'we examined the place from top to bottom. There just wasn't anywhere left where anybody could have hidden.'

'You stayed behind to do some correspondence, sir,' Denning remarked pensively. 'At what time did you finally leave?'

'About half an hour after you. Your men can verify that. I'm assuming they were on the job by then.'

'Yes, they were,' Denning agreed. 'Your leaving then after the rest of us was reported to me. And anybody else knocking about would have been seen . . . Hmmm.'

'*That* place,' Dr. Carruthers said, stirring at last, 'was prepared by somebody *after* we had examined it! The glimpse we had of the blazing ground floor was proof of it. It went up like a torch. There was also the smell of burning paraffin — I get used to differentiating between smells in my business. The person who arranged that fire must have saturated all the ground floor exhibits in paraffin and then let a fire-starting device operate at twelve o'clock, or just after.'

'That's just what we've been saying, isn't it?' Granwell demanded impatiently. 'But how could anybody have got in or out?'

'That doesn't concern me,' Carruthers shrugged. 'I'm a physicist, not a policeman — thank God. I'm merely drawing conclusions, and with everything on the ground floor drenched in paraffin the place naturally went up like a fire-cracker.'

'In that case,' Denning said, 'perhaps there'll be some remains of the fire-making device in the ashes.'

'I doubt it. One very simple method is to use a lighted candle standing in hay, which ignites the hay when it burns down to it. Another is to make a train of tinder — or maybe celluloid — on the floor from a candle, ending at the paraffin-soaked goods nearby. The flame of the candle would of course be shielded from the windows by some object or other. There are dozens of ways of starting a fire — and you'll find most of them tabulated by Hans Gross, if you're interested . . . Photographic film and paraffin drums were both in that store of yours, Mr. Granwell.'

'Yes,' Granwell admitted. 'Drums in the basement and films on the counter on the top floor.'

'Which makes our chances of finding a fire-raising device look pretty sick,' Grant muttered. 'It seems funny too that this thing tonight was a straightforward fire, whereas Bilkin suffered a terrific, baffling explosion.'

'I'm sick of just theories!' Granwell snapped. 'Either get some satisfactory investigation under way, Superintendent, or I'm going to see the Chief Constable and tell him I want Scotland Yard brought in . . . Good morning!'

He strode out of the office angrily and slammed the door. There was silence for a moment, then the detective-sergeant gave a slow, puzzled smile.

'I wonder,' he said, 'if *he* had anything to do with it?'

'I'd thought of that,' Denning muttered. 'But why should a man burn down his business and stand to perhaps lose the insurance as well? That isn't motive, it's plain lunacy. What do you think, Doctor?'

'I don't think anything, that's your job. What I am thinking about, and have been ever since first hearing about it, is that the ice delivered to Bilkin was yellow, wrapped in felt, and handled with exaggerated care. The dim glimmering of an idea is at last beginning to form. I'm going to try an experiment and find out. How about you coming over to my place at eleven in the morning?'

'Make it afternoon, sir,' Denning said. 'I have to attend the inquest on Bilkin in the morning. We'll ask for an adjournment, of course . . . Then I'll have a lot of details to attend to in regard to this emporium business. There is also an interview I have just got to have with Jones.'

'How can you do that now, sir?' Grant asked. 'We didn't get his address — '

'We can easily do it through the Labour Exchange,' Denning told him.

'Then be at my place about two-thirty,' Carruthers said, getting to his feet. 'I'll make time to look through the emporium debris for some sort of clue, even though I don't expect to find anything. Meantime let's get back home and grab some sleep. There's little enough of the night left . . . Come on, Gordon.'

* * *

Restored somewhat by two hours' sleep, Denning returned to the police station at nine in the morning to find that Grant had also returned to duty and was busy interviewing Amos Ballam, the fire assessor. He had done it so thoroughly, in fact, that Denning had no need to ask any further questions.

The fire assessor's findings were similar to the case of Bilkin. There was nothing to show that the fire had not been an accident and he intended making a claim. What legal chicanery he intended to practice he did not of course divulge.

Ballam had hardly departed en route to Granwell's home with his report before the Chief Constable arrived demanding to know what Denning intended to do next.

The genial Colonel's faith was under a severe strain — he was now anxious to call in Scotland Yard — but Denning, remembering Carruthers' somewhat ambiguous reference to yellow ice and its possibilities, clung to his point and finally succeeded — partially anyway — in convincing the Chief Constable that he could still handle matters, that developments would soon be forthcoming. Colonel Barrow finally agreed to delay calling in the Yard — for twenty-four hours.

These details polished off Denning contacted the Labour Exchange, secured the address of Stuart Jones from their files, and promptly dispatched the detective-sergeant to interview him. It was probable, in common with the rest of the emporium's staff, that the young man would be at his home, or rooms, waiting to see what Granwell would do next for his work-bereft employees.

Altogether Denning found himself with half an hour to spare, allowing him ample time to motor over to Werton where the inquest on Oscar Bilkin was to be held. He wondered if Mrs. Bilkin and her daughter had left the hospital yet. It was highly probable. If so, after the inquest, he resolved to ask them more questions about the ice block, which information might help Dr. Carruthers' investigations.

Denning left the police station, notifying the sergeant-in-charge of his intentions, and went out to his car. Then he gazed across the road at the hollow shell of the emporium. A small figure in a black homberg and overcoat, and the taller one of Gordon Drew, were visible — and with them a slender girl. They were standing a little apart from the inquisitive crowd surveying the ruins from the limitations imposed by the policemen.

Also amongst the crowd, though Denning was not aware of it, was a fluttering general manager detailed by Granwell to advise employees as they arrived that at a later date they would receive his instructions concerning their employment. By this time most of them had come and gone — Stuart Jones amongst them — but a few remained to survey or engage in gossip.

'Hello there, Denning!' Carruthers greeted, as the superintendent came up. 'How are things going this morning?'

'So-so,' Denning answered, then greeted Gordon and Janice Lloyd.

'I'm just going to start poking round,' Carruthers explained. 'I don't expect to find much though . . . You haven't forgotten our appointment for this afternoon?'

'It's about the only thing I'm looking forward to.'

Janice Lloyd, who had been contemplating the ruins, looked at Denning and gave a sigh. 'Things are getting worse in this town, Superintendent, don't you think? All that beautiful emporium gone up in smoke! It's giving poor Father a terrible time,' she added. 'Being the Borough Surveyor.'

'Why?' Denning asked curiously.

'It's a bit complicated,' Janice apologized. 'Just as I told Dr. Carruthers the other day when he asked the same question . . . You see, the destruction of Bilkin's fish-shop altered the value of the land round here — and now the end of the emporium alters it still more. Sorry to be vague, but I don't pretend to understand the workings of a Borough Surveyor's office. All I know is that these two disasters have piled a whole mass of work on Dad's department and he in particular is highly bothered about the whole thing. Matter of fact that's why I'm here. He's too busy to more than glance at the ruin on his way to the office. He asked me to have a look and see if I could find out how great the damage is — if the building is entirely gutted. It is — obviously . . . '

Denning looked at the sagging walls of the building adjoining the emporium shell. It had been gutted almost as completely as its neighbour.

'What's left will be pulled down — naturally,' he said, then paused as a spruce, elderly man with a pink, affable face made his presence felt. He was dressed in a dark overcoat and bowler hat and there was something about him that smelled of insurance.

'Superintendent Denning?' he enquired.

Denning nodded. 'You, I take it, are the assessor from the Allied and Industrial Insurance Trust?'

'That's right. Douglas Cloud's the name. I have to examine this, on behalf of my company. Mr. Granwell notified us . . . '

He came to a stop, his eyes on Gordon Drew. For a moment plain surprise crossed his features, then he gave an enigmatic smile. 'Mr. Drew, isn't it?' he asked quietly.

'Yes,' Gordon acknowledged tautly.

Denning was immediately alert. 'You two know each other?'

'Yes, indeed. Indeed we do!' Cloud gave an ambiguous laugh, but he did not commit himself any further.

'As a matter of police routine, Mr. Cloud,' Denning said, 'I'd be glad if you'd call at the police station down the road when you have finished your examination. I must have a record of the facts. If I don't happen to be there — I've an inquest in Werton to attend — I'd be glad if you'd wait. I shan't be long.'

'All right, Superintendent. I'll be along the moment I've finished here.'

Denning caught a stern, half-troubled look from Gordon Drew — then with a word of farewell he turned and went back to his car to commence the journey to the inquest.

* * *

The superintendent soon disposed of the inquest, securing an adjournment until the police enquiry was complete.

Mrs. Bilkin and her daughter, both of them fully recovered and garbed in black, were present, and Denning sought them out as they left the coroner's court.

'You're not doing so much to find my poor hubby's murderer are you, Superintendent?' were Mrs. Bilkin's opening words. 'In fact things seem to be getting worse! We've heard all about the emporium fire last night.'

By now, everybody in Halingford — and probably for a considerable distance round it — knew of the fire. Denning sidetracked the obviously accusing note in the woman's voice and instead came straight to the point he had in mind.

'Don't assume, Mrs. Bilkin, because there has been no actual arrest or published evidence as yet that we have been idle . . . I'm following quite a few lines of enquiry. At the moment you can be a big help to me — or at least you can, Miss Bilkin. For various reasons, that block of ice that was delivered to you has come into the picture again and I'd be glad of a few more particulars regarding it. I believe you described it as being yellowish? What exact colour of yellow?'

'Oh —' Edith Bilkin gestured vaguely. 'Pale yellow. Like weak tea or lemonade. Sometimes when we got an ice-block which was not of very clear water it looked very similar — only perhaps not quite as yellow as that one was.'

'What size was it?'

'Standard size — that is, three feet long by two wide by half a foot thick.'

Denning made a note. Then: 'And

didn't you say that your father used to break it up with a hammer and chisel?'

'That's right,' Edith assented, wondering. 'Every morning. He liked to smash it up into little bits — make a sort of carpet of it on the slab — and then he laid the fish cuts on it. What's so remarkable about that?'

'In itself, nothing.' Denning did not elaborate. Instead he asked: 'And there's nothing else you can think of concerning that ice? About the new ice-man, for instance? About the care with which he handled the block?'

But apparently the fount of information was exhausted, for neither the girl nor her mother had anything further to tell.

'How is your insurance claim proceeding?' Denning enquired.

'So far we haven't heard anything more,' Mrs. Bilkin replied. 'Mr. Ballam seemed quite sure we'd have the claim paid — in spite of that warning — and Mr. Vincent for the company was just as sure we wouldn't! So I suppose they'll argue it out between them.'

'Just so,' Denning agreed. 'When you

do hear something definite I'd be glad if you'd notify me.'

His questioning at an end Denning gave both women a lift in his car back to Halingford, left them at the corner of Larch Avenue, and then drove on to the police station. Douglas Cloud, the insurance company's assessor, was waiting in his office, talking to Grant.

'Sorry to have kept you waiting, Mr. Cloud,' Denning apologized, settling at his desk. 'I'd like to know if you have found anything on the site of the emporium fire?'

Douglas Cloud gave that peculiarly ambiguous laugh he had. 'I certainly have! For instance — two fire-warped drums that had previously contained paraffin. The smell of it is still in them.'

'Those would be from the basement stockroom,' Denning answered, remembering. 'I presume they will affect Mr. Granwell's insurance claim?'

'They will naturally be taken into account — but the final verdict rests with the company. You see, Mr. Granwell's policy is no ordinary one; it's full of technicalities and details that as yet I haven't had the chance to thoroughly examine. Another thing my company will have to take into full consideration is the warning note that Mr. Granwell received beforehand. That complicates things.

'Take a look,' Cloud added dryly at Denning's puzzled expression, and handed over the morning paper at the stop-press oblong. Denning, who had not seen this late issue of the London daily, scowled at the blue print:

ANOTHER MYSTERY FIRE

Following a printed warning to the owner, a disastrous fire occurred in Halingford last night. A fishmonger in the same town received similar warning a few days ago and was killed in the resultant wrecking of his premises.

'Fires, of which warning is given, do not occur by accident,' Cloud pointed out.

Grim-faced, Denning handed the

newspaper back. Granwell had said the letter had been in his morning mail. The sorting clerk must have seen it — so must the postman — so too must the sorters at Halingford post office.

Any of them, already aware that the Bilkin affair had started with a similar warning, could have talked to the local *Gazette* for a 'consideration'. The *Gazette*, in turn, could have passed the information on to the London news agencies.

'Nothing sacred,' Denning muttered to himself, then he looked at Douglas Cloud again as he moved restlessly in an obvious desire to depart. 'You know Mr. Drew, it seems? Would you mind telling me where you made his acquaintance?'

'As a matter of fact,' Cloud said slowly, 'it was in court. It concerned a claim for insurance.'

'Am I right in thinking, Mr. Cloud, that Mr. Drew's presence in this town is considerably influencing your mind in regard to Mr. Granwell's claim?'

'Naturally I cannot help but draw conclusions, and I shall have to mention them to my superiors. Candidly, however, it is not so much Drew who is influencing my opinion as that warning note. If anything kills Mr. Granwell's claim it will be that — with the presence of Drew for good measure.'

'I'd like to know more about Drew,' Denning said bluntly.

'Very well. Mr. Drew's business — Electrical Products Limited — was burned to the ground by fire and he lodged a claim with our company. The policy was not honoured because there were doubts as to its validity, and the court upheld those doubts. So the outcome was that the company won its case.'

'Are you trying to tell me that the fire at Drew's place was not deemed to have been caused by an accident?' Denning asked deliberately.

'Yes — but there wasn't enough evidence to show that there had actually been arson. No case could be brought against Drew, even though his claim was not considered valid. When I saw him this morning in Halingford I got quite a surprise.'

Denning got to his feet. 'Well, thank

you, Mr. Cloud. Your information will be of great help to me. Sorry to have detained you.'

After Cloud had taken his departure, Denning turned back to Grant. 'Did you see Jones?' he asked.

'I did sir — and got quite a lot of information out of him.' The detective-sergeant pulled out his notebook. 'I've got the full statement here and I'll type it out later and have Jones sign it. Would you like the gist now?'

'If you would.'

'First I managed to find the name of Ross's girl friend. She is Claire Denbury, a chorus girl, and at the moment is in a revue called 'Reach Me Down' which this week is playing in Birmingham.'

'I take it that Ross has told Jones all this?'

'Yes — Ross seems to have been quite proud of the fact that his girl friend is a stage performer. Your guess was right.'

'All right, go on. What else?'

'All those facts about Ross being utterly fed up with his quarters in the dispensary were quite true. And he did go to tackle

Granwell about it. He went up at half past five last Monday afternoon, at which time — according to Jones — the boss is usually alone, having completed his normal routine work. Apparently Ross did not explain why he had not actually seen Granwell. But he had a strange look on his face when he came back into the dispensary — as though he'd seen a ghost, was how Jones put it.'

'Did you ask Jones if he'd noticed that *Gazette*?' Denning asked briefly.

'I did — as tactfully as possible. He said he was prepared to swear that the bin was empty during the morning.'

Denning frowned. 'That's confoundedly odd. What else did you gather from him? Anything to suggest that he might be the guilty party?'

'No, sir, I didn't gather that impression.'

Denning sat thinking, then: 'I suppose Ross didn't give Jones any hint that he was intending to clear out?'

'No. Jones said it was as big a surprise to him as it seems to have been to everybody else.' Grant went through his notes and then added: 'Oh yes, one other thing! Ross believed that Granwell could not provide better quarters because it isn't possible to build another emporium in this district. Something to do with a legal clause that ties up the property. Jones was very hazy about it . . . '

'Then if Granwell couldn't provide better quarters, and Ross knew it, why on earth did he attempt to tackle him about it?' Denning mused. 'Unless he had the idea of emptying those storerooms and making more room that way. Incidentally, that business about the property being tied up has set me thinking of what Miss Lloyd had to say this morning. About the value of the land altering because the fish-shop and emporium have been destroyed. I think I'd better have a talk with the Borough Surveyor and see what he can tell me . . . '

'Apparently Ross had read about the legal tie-up in the reports in council meetings,' Grant added. 'As near as Jones could tell me there are three areas in Halingford which, as long as they have property on each of them, makes it impossible for any other plot of land to be bought for extensions or anything. One of those tomfool clauses you get in a land act sometimes, I suppose.'

Denning sat down, an abstracted look in his eyes. Out of the whole tangled confusion the dim outlines of a positive motive were beginning to appear, but as yet there was no means by which he could develop his idea. One man could — the Borough Surveyor, and he made a mental note to interview him at the earliest possible moment.

'That's about all I got out of Jones,' Grant said, closing up his notebook. 'I believe that Ross went to Birmingham when he left Halingford. Only,' Grant added, frowning, 'that doesn't link up with the note being sent to Granwell, presumably by Ross, nor have we an explanation for the *Gazette* in the waste bin. I cannot think that he would be crazy enough to leave the cut-up *Gazette* for anybody to see, any more than Ross would.'

'Whether Ross went to Birmingham or not, it's likely that this girl Claire

Denbury might know of his movements,' Denning reached for the telephone. 'I'll get the Birmingham police to contact her. I've got to interview her at the earliest moment. They'll trace her from that revue. What was it called again?'

''Reach Me Down', sir.'

Grant waited until his superior had finished his conversation with Birmingham police headquarters — then he asked a question.

'I suppose we're on the right track in suspecting Ross, sir? In view of what that chap Cloud had to say about Mr. Drew?''

'That came as a definite shock to me,' Denning admitted. 'It may only be circumstantial. If we followed it up we might make a mess of things. Though it seems Drew was mixed up in a case of arson we have, in these local affairs, several things to remember. Being an assistant to Dr. Carruthers, Drew had no chance to arrange any dirty work, and even less opportunity to send the warnings. Further, unlike Ross, he didn't try to escape from Halingford. Weighed against that is Drew's summing-up of the property on the day he came to Halingford, and the fact that he knows this town intimately.

'Even if he was wanting to maybe wipe off old scores — as far as Bilkin was concerned — that doesn't apply in the case of Granwell since he is a recent arrival. So, until we have something more, I'll limit myself to questions with Mr. Drew and decide later whether or not he'll bear stronger investigation. I still think that it's *Ross* we want: he's a chemist, he had a possible motive, and he has disappeared . . . '

Denning did not consider he was called upon to commit himself any further at that moment and so he said nothing of the other little bits and pieces that were formed at the back of his mind.

Why, for instance, had Clayton Ross needed to 'look like a ghost' after going to tackle his employer upon a matter on which his — Ross's — mind was fully made up? A sensitive person might have quailed and gone paler at the last moment, but not a man of the type of the head dispenser.

And why had the man been such a fool as to leave the *Gazette* in the waste bin? Why, despite the change in the face of Halingford, had the Borough Surveyor such need to be 'worried to death', as his daughter had put it? Was it as important as all that?

These were the major questions drifting unanswered in Denning's mind, while the minor ones resolved into — curved nail scissors, the puzzling burn scar on the face of Gordon Drew, and . . .

One point nearly linked up for a moment. Granwell had been reading the *Halingford Gazette* when he, Denning, had called upon him in his office concerning Ross. Perhaps, then . . .

But there was no room for 'perhaps' in his profession — and Denning well knew it. He glanced at the clock — it was 12.15 — and then back to Grant.

'Granwell hasn't been in, I suppose?'

'Apparently not, sir, I suppose he is waiting for us to make the next move. He'll have plenty on his plate, I imagine, deciding how to get his business on its feet again.'

Denning nodded and then picked up the telephone. A brief conversation with the Borough Surveyor's office assured him that that gentleman had departed for lunch and would not be back until two.

'You might tell him I'll do my best to call on him some time this afternoon,' Denning said, and hung up.

'The Borough Surveyor, sir?' Grant asked, curiously. 'You surely don't think that he fits into it? He's about one of the most respected men in the community.'

'I'm just interested in the fact that he's worried over these disasters which keep occurring. Why should he need to be? I believe that a word or two with him might help to clear up a lot of things. For the moment I think we'd better get some lunch before seeing what Dr. Carruthers has in store for us.'

12

Arriving at the little scientist's home exactly on time Denning and the detective-sergeant found him apparently ready and waiting.

Gordon Drew, quiet and attentive to Carruther's every wish, nodded to them as they entered the Den. Denning had made up his mind to ask Gordon many questions — but that could wait until later.

'Well, Superintendent,' Carruthers said, 'I think I've got something for you at last. It's the outcome of eliminating every other possibility — the only way to arrive at an incontrovertible scientific conclusion.'

Denning said nothing, awed by the man's pedantry.

'That being so, let's go below.'

Carruthers led the way out of the Den and down the steps into the well-lighted laboratory. Motioning the two policemen — and Gordon Drew — to halt when they had half crossed the basement, he himself continued to a further wall and pointed to a bench.

Upon it stood a structure rather like a miniature pile-driver. Denning was reminded for a moment of a Heath Robinson sketch he had seen somewhere.

'I intend to demonstrate what I believe caused the destruction of Bilkin's fish-shop,' Carruthers explained, enjoying himself. 'Here is a heavy lead weight suspended by a cord. When I pull this cord from a distance the weight will drop hard upon . . . '

He turned to a refrigerator and opened the door, taking from it a small cube of what appeared to be yellowish ice. He removed it carefully from the lowest shelf, using a small piece of felt for the purpose. The cube, Denning noticed, was about an inch square, rather like a golden-coloured lump of camphor.

'This,' Carruthers explained, 'is a small scale sample of the ice delivered to Mr. Bilkin — or so I believe. Now watch!'

He placed the cube at the base of the 'pile-driver' device, directly under the suspended lead weight, and then stepped back with the length of green blind cord trailing from his hand. Suddenly he jerked the cord. Denning, the detective-sergeant, and Drew had a momentary vision of the lead weight dropping — then there was a blinding flash and a report that stung their eardrums in the confined space . . .

There was a wave of hot air and a tinkling of delicate instruments, then except for a dispersing cloud of evil-smelling smoke the business was over. But the 'pile-driver' gadget had entirely disappeared and one or two bottles at the back of the bench had been broken in the experiment.

Denning pinched his eyes for a moment as he saw bright spots in front of them, 'What happened? What was it?'

Carruthers chuckled, feeling just like a magician who has performed an extra good trick. 'What was it? Why, our old friend nitro-glycerin.'

Denning frowned, calling to mind his schoolboy chemistry lessons. 'But that is a kind of oily fluid — '

'And it is amber yellow,' Carruthers reminded him. 'Nitro-glycerin is also one of the simplest things in the world to freeze. It becomes a crystalline mass hardly distinguishable from ice of yellow colour — but it takes a good chemist to do it. In its frozen form the merest tap causes it to detonate with terrific violence. You saw what happened to that small cube? A block the size of Bilkin's ice-block would obviously explode with shattering force when struck with a hammer and chisel.'

'My God!' Denning said. 'That block was three feet by two and six inches thick!'

'What you have just witnessed was an exact re-enactment of what we might melodramatically call 'The Death of Bilkin',' Carruthers remarked dryly. 'When I weighed up all the facts, I came up with the solution to his mysterious death.

'In the first place, this ice-man had the block wrapped in felt — an unusual precaution; for another, Miss Bilkin said that he treated the block as tenderly as a baby — and also it appears that the ice-man departed with an almost indecent haste. The morning was bitterly cold and frosty. There was no chance of the frozen nitro-glycerin melting before its deadly work was done. The moment Bilkin hit it the block exploded with stupendous violence.

'The wonder is that he wasn't blown to pieces, but then you can never tell with blast. It creates the most extraordinary conditions for itself, and a lot would depend on exactly where Bilkin had the block when he started to break it. Somehow or other he missed being resolved into atoms and received terrible and fatal injuries instead.'

Carruthers was right, Denning decided, because nothing else fitted it. But he was nevertheless astounded by the fiendish ingenuity behind it.

'Somebody, then, knew that Bilkin was in the habit of smashing the ice with hammer and chisel,' he said.

'Almost anybody in Halingford might be aware of it, sir,' Grant commented. 'On my way to the police-station I've often seen him smashing it up before the day's sales.'

'There is also another point,' Carruthers added, 'The unknown also knew — no doubt from the weather forecasts — that the weather was likely to remain cold and frosty so there would be little chance of the ice-block melting before it reached its destination.'

'Then this must mean that whoever sent that note was not the same person who planned the deed,' Denning said, pondering.

Carruthers nodded his Beethovian head. 'What you mean is that had Bilkin taken the hint to depart he would not have been there either to receive or smash up the ice? Hence no explosion. Right?'

'That's right,' Denning assented. 'I've got to get in touch with the Cold Ice Company immediately and find out what's going on. The driver who took the ice to Bilkin must be closely questioned.' Denning turned sharply. 'Grant, hop over to 22 Larch Avenue and see Miss Bilkin. I didn't get a description of the ice-man from her because at that time I didn't see that it signified. Get her to give you every detail about him — and his name if she knows it. Quickly as you can.'

As the detective-sergeant departed Denning looked again at Carruthers.

'You said that only a good chemist could work up a trick like this, sir?'

'No doubt of it. Freezing nitro-glycerin is a slow and ticklish business — and blasted dangerous, but it is not beyond the capabilities of any skilled chemist.'

'Like Ross? Or Jones?'

'I imagine they'd be capable of it,' the scientist agreed. 'And since there were considerable quantities of glycerin and nitric acid in the dispensary — from which nitro-glycerin is made, of course — and a refrigerator plant, it would not be beyond either of them to create a frozen block of nitro-glycerin.'

'The nerve of that ice-man!' Denning whistled. 'To drive his truck with frozen nitro-glycerin upon it!'

'How he was inveigled into delivering it we don't know,' Carruthers said. 'But it's quite possible he did not know what the stuff was, otherwise I don't think his nerve would have been up to it.'

'But he delivered it wrapped in felt and

handled it with exceptional care,' Denning objected.

'He could have been told to handle it very carefully — and did so, but even then he didn't really know what the stuff was.'

'Mmm — yes.' Denning mused, then: 'The Cold Ice Company is in Werton — I know that — and the road from there to Halingford isn't too good either. Too much bumping might have exploded that nitro-glycerin. That seems to indicate that it was only brought a very short distance, and along smooth road at that.'

'The van moved at funeral pace and braked gently,' Carruthers reminded him. 'Or so you said when relating Miss Bilkin's story.'

'It *could* have come only a few yards with that particular block! From as far as the emporium, for instance! If Ross or Jones or somebody were there — ' Denning broke off, realizing he was getting ahead of his evidence. 'But whoever planned it had the devil of a nerve. Supposing the thing had blown up before accomplishing its purpose?'

'That risk had to be taken, of course,' Carruthers admitted. 'But with that felting and other precautions, the risk wasn't great. Had the worst happened and the ice-man and his truck been blown up, the plotter would have worked out some other scheme.'

Denning reflected that the ice-man might have had some obscure reason for blowing up the fish-shop, yes — but what about the emporium?

'Do you think, Doctor,' he asked, 'that the emporium disaster was caused by a similar scientific process?'

'Not for one moment. It was a straightforward fire, and probably started by candle and celluloid, helped on its way by paraffin.'

'I see. Well — many thanks.' Denning gave Gordon a casual glance. 'What do you think of this nitro-glycerin angle? Would you say that it is chemically possible?'

'I can't think of any reason why not,' Gordon answered frankly. 'And if Dr. Carruthers says so that's good enough for me.'

'I take it then that you are something of a chemist yourself, Mr. Drew?' Denning asked shrewdly.

'Hardly that. I've no degrees for it, if that's what you mean. You might call me an unprofessional chemist — and add to it a fair smattering of general knowledge.'

'Do you mind if I ask you a rather personal question — privately?' Denning persisted.

Gordon smiled. 'There's no need for privacy. I don't mind Dr. Carruthers knowing anything. What's your question?'

'All right. Is it correct that your business of Electrical Products was destroyed by fire, about which there was something . . . not quite regular? That your claim was turned down by the Allied and Industrial Insurance Trust?'

'If you mean was arson suspected and was I supposed to be a fire-raiser — about which fact there was no real proof — yes!'

'I hope,' Denning said grimly, 'you realize the seriousness of what you are saying, in view of the fact that you studied the Bilkin property on the day you arrived in town?'

'You're exceeding your authority, Superintendent,' Gordon answered shortly. 'I guessed that this would come up when I noticed the way you looked at me and then Mr. Cloud this morning. You've obviously questioned him. I can't do a thing about that, but if you think I had anything to do with the Halingford disasters, you must be crazy!'

'In my job,' Denning said, 'I have to consider every aspect. You are a suspected fire-raiser, and a chemist in an unprofessional way. You took an unusual interest in a shop which was later destroyed, and — if I may become purely personal — a scar on your face which is obviously from burning and which you did not have when you left this town eight years ago.'

'All this speculation of yours is totally misplaced, Superintendent,' Carruthers growled. 'I knew all about Mr. Drew here when I asked him to consider being my assistant The facts of the Electrical Products fire, and his own part in it, were all in the *Sunday Illustrated* for December 2 last.'

'But you engaged Mr. Drew *before*

anything peculiar had happened in this town,' Denning pointed out.

'Oh dammit, man — ' Carruthers began impatiently, but Gordon himself interrupted.

'Look here, Superintendent, I'll tell you what actually happened, and after that it's up to you. In the firm of Electrical Products there were quite a few of my friends — who formed it into a limited company, but the one with the money-bags was a shady customer, though I didn't know it at the time. The enterprise lost money with monumental success. One night this partner of mine came to me with the calm admission — thinking that I was as unscrupulous as himself — that he had 'fixed' our business so it would go up in flames and we'd collect the insurance.

'Far from agreeing with his plot I tried to prevent it. I drove to the building as fast as I could go and almost managed to stop the fire-raising device from working — but not quite! I got badly burned — hence this scar on my face — and whilst in hospital it seems I babbled a lot about the fire-raising device. Statements uttered in delirium are no use as evidence, naturally, but it did get the assessors to work, Douglas Cloud among them, on behalf of the insurance company.

'Cloud found what he considered to be sufficient evidence to prove that the fire had been deliberately arranged — in the shape of tin trays, magnesium powder deposit, and so on, for I might add my partner was anything but an expert fire-raiser, and so, though I put in my claim, it was turned down flat. All I got was severe censure, with the suspicion but not the proof that I was an incendiary. Cleaned out, I finally came to Halingford to get the taste of unpleasant things out of my mouth and revive a few precious old memories.'

'And your fire-raising partner?' Denning questioned.

'He disappeared when he knew I was going to stop the fire — and the rest of my friends, fearful of being implicated, did likewise. I haven't the remotest idea where they are, nor, I think, have the police. That is why I got the whole brunt of responsibility.'

'Well, I wish you'd have told me this sooner,' Denning said.

'I suppose I have been a bit of a fool in keeping it so much to myself,' Gordon said, 'but when I saw what was happening in Halingford here I realized just how much suspicion would attach to me, so I kept quiet. I haven't explained a word to Miss Lloyd, either, though I know she's consumed with curiosity to know how I came by this scar on my face. One of these days I'll tell her . . . when this business is all cleared up. You can check back on my story if you like.'

'No need,' Denning said simply. 'I have your word, and Dr. Carruthers is prepared to vouch for you. I'm trying to eliminate suspects, not create them. You're off the list. Sorry if I doubted you, but it's all part of my job.'

'Thanks,' Gordon Drew said, smiling.

Denning glanced at his watch. 'I must be getting along, sir,' he said, looking at Carruthers. 'I'm more than obliged for your help. I'll let you know what develops next.'

* * *

Denning returned to the police station, and found that Detective-Sergeant Grant had completed his enquiries of Miss Bilkin and was typing out the relative facts of the case as they had so far been gathered.

'Any luck?' Denning asked, as Grant got up and followed him into his office.

'Yes sir — full description. About five feet four, very broad-shouldered, square-faced, and eyes that might be blue or grey. Reefer overcoat with a high collar and a fawn-coloured cap. No name. Miss Bilkin never asked it him and naturally he didn't give it.'

Grant handed over a sheet from his scratchpad upon which he had written the description in detail. Denning nodded, and put it in his wallet.

'I'll go over to the Cold Ice Company and see what they can tell me,' he said. 'After I've seen the Borough Surveyor. Mrs. Bilkin say anything else?'

'Yes,' Grant replied. 'Her insurance claim has been turned down flat. She's very bitter about it.'

'Understandable,' Denning sighed. 'However, it may be possible for something to be done later when it is seen that she and her daughter are the helpless victims of a vicious attack. Meanwhile we have even more important things on our mind. After you left I had a talk with our Gordon Drew, and I think we can now rule him out.'

Grant looked dubious, but when he had heard all the facts he nodded slowly. 'Yes, that seems conclusive enough,' he agreed.

'It also appears,' Denning said, 'that we may be wrong in suspecting Ross as the culprit, for if he sent the note he automatically could not be. It would have killed his own plot stone dead . . . '

'Do you think that perhaps — if we assume Ross plotted the whole thing — he got the wind up at what he'd done and tried to stop it by sending a warning to get out?'

'That,' Denning said, 'doesn't take into account certain other facts. The note reached Bilkin the day before the tragedy happened, yet, obviously according to plan, the ice-man arrived on the fatal morning. If Ross had been aware so much earlier that he was going to scotch his plan why did he allow the ice to be delivered?'

'Perhaps he couldn't stop it because he'd planned it a long way beforehand?'

'No. That lorry only travelled a very short distance,' Denning said. 'To travel a long way with a cargo like that would have been too dangerous, and cold though the air was, melting might have taken place by very reason of the felt being wrapped round it.

'So I incline to the idea that the 'ice' was taken from a refrigerator, put on the lorry, and delivered almost immediately. Had Ross wanted to stop the whole thing he had plenty of time . . . No, I'm sure he sent a warning — and nothing more.'

'Then why the devil did he clear off?'

'As to that . . . excuse me!' Denning turned to the shrilling telephone. 'Yes? Halingford police — Superintendent Denning speaking . . . She can't be moved? In hospital? Oh, blast! Yes, of course.' Denning gave a sigh. 'I quite understand . . . keep me notified. It's most urgent. Right . . . Goodbye.'

Grant glanced at him questioningly.

'That was Birmingham police headquarters. Claire Denbury is in Birmingham General Hospital — been taken ill with appendicitis. They're operating today. We shan't get a word out of her until tomorrow at the earliest — and then it will be in the hospital.'

Denning picked up his uniform cap again. 'I'll go along and see the Borough Surveyor and then the Cold Ice Company. Then — '

Denning stopped as the sergeant-in-charge knocked and announced Mr. Granwell. The bitterness of his mood showed in his flinty glance and the jut of his jaw.

Apparently his distress was not so great, however, that he had neglected his appearance. He was faultlessly dressed in dark grey, his overcoat adorned with a carnation in the lapel.

'Good afternoon, Mr. Granwell,' Denning greeted.

Granwell did not return the welcome. 'How much longer are you going to clown about with this business, Denning? First Bilkin, now my place — and not a thing done! I'm going to ask the Chief Constable to call in Scotland Yard . . . Dammit, you're simply standing still!'

'As a matter of fact I'm making quite good progress,' Denning answered. 'Enough anyway to satisfy the Chief Constable for the time being. Actual results will probably be here in a matter of hours.'

'Matter of hours!' Granwell repeated sourly. 'My business in ruins and all I get are promises. It may interest you to know that I have spent my time until now arguing the emporium fire with the insurance company.'

'With what result, sir?' Denning questioned.

'The right one, of course!' Granwell sat down decisively and put his hat on the end of the desk. 'My claim — worked out by Amos Ballam — will be paid in full.'

'Oh? It will?' Denning frowned. 'Then I congratulate you, Mr. Granwell. You've certainly done better than Mrs. Bilkin.

I've just heard from her that her claim has been disallowed because of the clearly deliberate nature of the fire.'

'That,' Granwell answered, shrugging, 'is her hard luck. Her husband, if it was he who arranged the policy, should have considered more carefully what kind of a policy he was taking out. Mine covers a use and occupancy clause whereby my entire goodwill and stock has been lost, and profits wiped out. That will be made good. I have also a variation of the fidelity insurance that guards me against wrongful acts by outside persons. In a word, my insurance is that of a businessman. I don't lose anything — which is a big relief to me. Of course, though, I've a lot of work ahead of me to get the place rebuilt. So many restrictions to be overcome, But they can be . . . and will be!'

'Yes, of course.' Denning spoke absently, his mind on something else. Then, 'If you are taken care of by your insurance, Mr. Granwell, why do you find it necessary to pitch into me?'

'Well, you don't think any amount of money is much compensation for a place such as my emporium was, do you? Besides, I want to see the miscreant arrested before I start making any fresh plans. I'm not taking the risk of more disasters when I start rebuilding. Somebody has it in for me, as they had for Bilkin. So the sooner you get busy, the better. Who have you in mind? Clayton Ross? If you haven't you should have!'

'I've many lines of enquiry,' Denning answered ambiguously.

Granwell demurred and then finally shrugged his heavy shoulders. 'Maybe I'm being a bit unfair. Not seeing you in action I jump to the natural conclusion that nothing is being done . . . But whatever you *are* doing, make it quick. If you don't . . . well, I have enough authority in this town to get you short shrift.' He nodded curtly, picked up his hat, and went out of the office.

'No wonder Ross doesn't like him,' the detective-sergeant commented; 'even though I can see his point of view.'

'No wonder,' Denning agreed, buttoning the lowest button of his tunic jacket. 'You'd better stay and see if anything turns up, Grant. I'm on my way to the Borough Surveyor and the Cold Ice Company.'

Denning left the office, got into his car, and drove the few hundred yards down the High Street, which finally brought him to the grey bulk of the municipal offices. On the top floor of the Borough Surveyor's department a girl clerk ushered him into the presence of the gentleman himself.

Geoffrey Lloyd was a big, bluff, fair-headed man. He looked worried, even though his smile was cordial enough as he shook the superintendent's hand.

'Glad you dropped in, Superintendent. I've been expecting you after your message. You've come about these disasters in the town, I imagine.'

'That's right, sir. We police have to consider every angle . . . First. Would you mind telling me why these disasters worry you so much? Your daughter has mentioned to me that they are causing you a good deal of anxiety.'

Lloyd smiled faintly. 'Yes, she said that she had been chatting to you — and as regards myself she's right. The worry to me is that there may be more trouble yet, on top of that which has already occurred. You see, if things get any worse I might lose my job because of it. That's enough to make any man worried, isn't it?'

'You've mentioned *more* trouble. Where exactly?'

'Possibly — there!' The Borough Surveyor got to his feet and indicated the wall map behind him. It showed Halingford Road and his finger rested on a spot which was set opposite, and midway between, the points which had formerly been occupied by Bilkin's shop, and the shop immediately adjoining Granwell's corner emporium — and which, like the emporium, had now been gutted. Denning got to his feet and walked across the office to study the map more attentively.

'That's where there is a small teashop and confectioner, isn't it?' he asked.

'Not quite. The exact focal point is Bedford's, the florist's. Do you notice anything significant about these three points? Bilkin, the shop next to the emporium, and the florists?'

Denning mused and then answered. 'It suggests to me a triangle. If we call Granwell's Emporium point 'A' of the base line, Bilkin's point 'B', and the florists point 'C', as the apex.'

'Exactly — a triangle,' Lloyd agreed moodily. 'That's the trouble, believe me!'

He motioned back to the chairs again and settled heavily at the desk. 'You see,' Lloyd said slowly, 'all the land for quarter of a mile around the area created by that metaphorical triangle is bound up in a legal clause, dating back to God knows when. Stated briefly, it means that no land in the area I've mentioned can be used for the purpose of erecting a building if the erection of that building means knocking down any of the existing property. You follow?'

'I do,' Denning agreed. 'Does that account for the somewhat antique appearance of the High Street?'

'It does. It is one of those clauses that interfere with progress, but the legal technicalities are such that, though we have tried, we cannot get them altered.

The original idea — to safeguard the owners of the property within that area — has long since outlived its usefulness. In these modern days of advancement and new architecture it has the opposite effect. We cannot even condemn the property in that area. It must remain as it is, to fall or otherwise collapse until the three designated points cease to be.'

'Two of which,' Denning said, 'have already gone — Bilkin's and, thanks to the fire at Granwell's, the adjoining building which formed the second point . . . And if the third should go, what would happen then?'

'It would mean that providing the right price is paid for the area of land bought, there would be nothing to stop anybody putting up any kind of building they liked.'

'No planning restrictions?' Denning asked.

'They are not rigid in this instance because no new building has been undertaken for years. There wouldn't be much difficulty about that. Any firm, providing they paid enough, could demand that the rest of the property in the High Street be knocked down on the grounds of age, and nothing would be able to stop it.'

'But surely the rights of the small traders are protected?'

'They would be allowed compensation, of course, but nothing more. There are no clauses in the land contract to protect them once those 'guardian points', as we call them, have gone. Some of the traders, I believe, know of these 'guardian points' and have basked for years in their safety. With them gone, anything can happen.'

'So,' Denning said, thinking, 'it means that somebody with sufficient power and monopoly — say a big chain-store firm — could literally buy up all that area in the High Street, on both sides, and erect their own multiple places on it, once the third 'guardian point' has gone?'

'That's it!' The Borough Surveyor looked bothered.

'Why should that fact cause you to worry? Surely the town would benefit by becoming modernized?'

'Outwardly, yes. I grant you that

streamlined buildings would look well — but just think for a moment . . . Do you realize what happens in a small town like this when a monopoly large enough to buy up the main street takes over? That monopoly becomes the town, and the members of the council merely puppets. It is commercial dictatorship, and I have little wish to become a slave to a monopoly, at its orders. As things stand I can work with a free hand for the good of the community generally, providing the council members agree with me, and also providing I work outside the 'guardian points' area.'

'How do you know a monopoly *would* take over?' Denning questioned. 'Couldn't the traders already here buy up the land?'

'They could — but the position is so obvious! Everybody knows that these two recent disasters have somehow been engineered. The papers are full of it. That can only mean that a powerful monopoly is behind the whole thing, and that saboteurs are being used. That same monopoly will buy up the 'body' when it has been destroyed.'

'It surprises me,' Denning said, frowning, 'that 'accidental' fires haven't been resorted to before now to be rid of these vital — er — flashpoints. An unscrupulous person might have done it long ago.'

'But didn't,' Lloyd pointed out, his mouth tightening. 'We have a sense of honour in the council, Superintendent, even if you doubt it!'

'I don't mean any offence: I'm merely stating a logical conjecture . . . However, you've certainly done a good deal to clear up my mind. I thought something of the kind might be at the back of it from what your daughter had to tell me — '

'Oh?' Lloyd interrupted sharply. 'What else did she tell you besides the fact that I'm worried?'

'She told me that certain parts of this town are tied up in legal clauses, which she doesn't understand. She remarked that you had mentioned the fact from time to time.'

'That's true — but it was not meant to go any further. It's official business . . . ' The Borough Surveyor gave a rather hard smile. 'I'm afraid I shall have to take that young lady to task.'

'No doubt,' Denning agreed coolly, getting to his feet. 'Thank you for your time. I'll let you know how we get on.'

He shook the Borough Surveyor's hand and left the office. In a thoughtful mood he drove his car on to Werton, turning over various possibilities in his mind as he went, fitting a complicated jigsaw into place, as the basis of the deep-laid scheme began to dawn upon him. But, convinced though he was of its correctness, there remained that one irritating but ruthless necessity of the law . . . proof.

13

The one trouble about Cornelius Bedford, the florist in Halingford Road, was his absentmindedness . . . at least in all matters in which he did not feel an imperative interest. Possibly this tendency to forgetfulness might have ruined his business entirely had he not long ago schooled himself in the art of making detailed notes of every order he received.

This process had commenced when on one occasion he had sent the wreaths for a funeral five days late, which oversight had not been appreciated by the customer or even perhaps by the corpse . . .

But, grave though this oversight had been, it had not been half so grave as the present blunder he had committed, for in his jacket pocket, as he pottered cheerfully about the steamy warmth of his shop, there was a printed warning, phrased in similar fashion to the warnings received by Oscar Bilkin and Rupert

Granwell and, likewise, cut from the titles in a newspaper.

In fact, Cornelius Bedford had forgotten all about the letter. He had found it delivered around noon through the shop doorway with a couple of invoices, had glanced briefly at the peculiarly arranged address and wondered vaguely where he had heard of something similar — then he had thrust it in his pocket without bothering to open it.

By this time — 4.30 in the afternoon — it was as remote in his mind as the first days in his cradle. Had he but read it he would have discovered that it differed from the previous notes in one essential. It did not give him warning to get out by the following day, but *immediately*.

So, blissfully unaware that he was working in an aura of danger — and the police department also in ignorance of the fact that 'Guardian Point No. 3' was now threatened — Mr. Cornelius Bedford continued his ministrations to an array of daffodils, violets, late chrysanthemums, and lilies.

He was a man who fitted perfectly into

his surroundings. Tall, slender as a willow, with sunken cheeks and grey hair. He was a bachelor of sixty-three, with no other interest in life outside his beloved plants. All other things which existed were on another plane of thought, as far as he was concerned, hence the lack of interest in the warning.

Though, somewhere at the back of his mind, he did remember that his shop had narrowly escaped destruction from blast in the Bilkin business, the black hole of which loomed diagonally across the road like an empty tooth. The occurrence had suggested to him at the time that perhaps he and the property ought to be insured — then the idea had faded just as quickly.

Business had not been very brisk during the morning — Mrs. Berrick to order a wreath for her departed brother-in-law; Mr. Granwell to order half a dozen bunches of daffodils for his wife and a carnation buttonhole for himself. Must have one, he had said. Was going to make an impression — On an insurance company.

So, always willing to oblige, Cornelius

Bedford had obtained the carnation from the rear quarters of his shop where the carnations, not then sorted or displayed, were stocked.

Friday was usually quiet, and Mr. Bedford was not particularly worried either. Like thousands of small traders he had the baffling knack of being able to keep going without any visible means of support, and surprisingly, he made a practice of closing promptly at five, instead of six like the rest of the shops.

What the rest of the people did not know — except his bank manager — was that Mr. Bedford was worth almost £500,000, the handsome legacy bestowed by a vagrant uncle who with an almost novelettish flavour had struck it rich in America and made his pile.

The fact explained how with his small clientele he could afford the exorbitant market-garden prices demanded for his rarer offerings few of which were ever purchased.

Came 4.55, and as usual at this moment Bedford went out of the front door and propped it open with a V-shaped wedge of wood between the tiled floor and the door base. Then he turned to the three-feet-high wire basket-stand that stood just inside the porchway, flush with the wall opposite the cracked side window.

In this stand, as always, were three fairly large red flowerpots containing those olive-green abominations with spikes seen in Western films.

Bedford preferred to bestow upon them the dignified names of *opuntia vulgaris*, *nopalea coccinellifera*, and *coccus cacti* respectively — but to the layman they were plainly and simply cactus, and about the only plants which seemed capable of withstanding the outer air without any visible signs of hurt.

Cornelius Bedford noticed that there was something unusual on the surface of the compost in which the cacti stood. It looked as though some bright lad had put several thin, flat lengths of pink toffee paper there, the kind in which some manufacturers wrap their more succulent products. They seemed to be half dug into the compost somehow . . .

The discovery checked Bedford's intention to grab hold of either end of the wire stand and haul it into the shop. Instead he plucked irritably at one of the papers, touched to the quick by this act of desecration. That his plants should become a refuse heap for toffee paper — !

Then it happened.

The instant he touched the paper the world ended for Mr. Cornelius Bedford. He had one transient vision of blinding violet fire. It exploded instantly in a concussion of hot air and smoke.

The already cracked windows buckled inwards and glass javelins hurtled into the midst of the tumbling floral exhibits. 'Wreaths Made to Order', still fastened to the green-painted trellis at the back of the window, blasted inwards into the shop.

Bedford himself, already atrociously burned, blinded, and helpless, was flung clean across the pavement and dropped senseless in the gutter.

Two passers-by — one a man with a carrier bag in his hand and the other a schoolgirl, found themselves dropped miraculously unhurt in the middle of the road, on their faces, both of them with the vision of a searing violet flame of unimaginable beauty imprinted on their retinas —

Then with a flash and a crackling roar the inflammable wood and light materials in the shop caught fire. Smoke began to pour into the grey light of the February afternoon . . .

⋆ ⋆ ⋆

Half an hour prior to these violent events Superintendent Denning had arrived back at the Halingford police station from his trip to the Cold Ice Company. He was doing his best to satisfy Detective-Sergeant Grant's intense curiosity.

'At least,' he said, settling at his desk, 'we're starting to make real progress, Grant. I spoke with the Cold Ice's general manager, and after a good deal of shenanigans it turned out that one of their regular men — Bill Higgins, which is the name of the usual ice-man as mentioned by Mrs. and Miss Bilkin, accepted a substantial bribe from a stranger who wanted to borrow his ice-truck for half an hour on the fatal morning.

'I saw Higgins himself,' Denning went on. 'Naturally he wasn't particularly free with his information, since it means the sack and also the threat of whatever the law may decide to do with him later, but it did come out that he's the gambling type, short of money for that reason, and saw no particular harm in picking up easy money for the trifling demand made upon him . . .

'The arrangement was made in the Horse and Foal in Werton where Higgins is a regular. The plan was for Higgins to drive his lorry — empty — to a pre-arranged spot just outside Werton for seven in the morning, sharp. A big, stiff tarpaulin was to be provided, so arranged as to make it look as though there were ice-blocks underneath it.

'Higgins explained to the yard foreman that he was starting early before collecting his load, so he could have some engine trouble fixed. The yard foreman had no reason to be suspicious. So, our square-shouldered friend — as described by Miss

Bilkin and Bill Higgins — took over the truck from the pre-arranged point in Werton, drove it to Halingford, collected his deadly cargo, delivered it forty-five minutes earlier than the usual time for the ice-man to call, and then drove the lorry back to Werton for the waiting Bill Higgins to pick it up and begin loading for his daily round — with the one exception that he was not to call on Bilkin.

'Square-shoulders spun the none-too-bright Higgins some tale about wanting the truck for a joke. However, Higgins has since heard about what happened in the Bilkin shop and although desperately alarmed about it, had been too scared to speak. I took down his statement in full . . .'

Denning laid it on the desk. 'Type it out later, Grant, and we'll have him sign it.'

'I will, sir. And this chap with the square shoulders? He can tell us everything we need to know, if we can find him.'

'*If* we can find him!' Denning grimaced. 'He is one very small fish in a very big pond. I can — and will — circulate his description in the hope that he may be picked up. He would certainly be well paid for the work he did and he's no doubt lying low at a spot far removed from Halingford. But I'm after much bigger fish . . . You see, Grant, there is no longer any doubt in my mind as to whom we have to blame for all this — '

Denning's sentence was suddenly truncated by the precipitate arrival of the sergeant-in-charge, a look of intense urgency on his beefy face.

'You'd better come, sir,' he said quickly. 'Explosion — or fire — or something, down the road. A schoolkid's just come in the station to tell us.'

Denning told Grant to ring for the fire brigade and ambulance, then he raced out into the outer office.

The schoolgirl who had been passing the florist's shop at the time of the explosion had, it seemed, more sense than the man with the carrier in his hand — unless he had been more dazed than she. Anyhow, he had got on his way after a frightened glance back at the sprawled figures of the girl and the florist, and the crackling fire in the shop.

Now, the youngster with holes in the knees of her stockings, dirt on her face and clothes, stood giving the grim-faced Denning her story.

'Right,' he said crisply, once he had gathered the details. 'You stay here awhile, m'dear, and your mother will be sent for . . . You're not badly hurt, are you?'

'No sir,' she whispered. 'Only — only my eyes hurt a bit from that awful purple flash I saw — '

'You'll be all right . . . Sergeant!'

'Sir?' The sergeant-in-charge hovered over the child.

'Keep your eye on this young lady. Get her address and send for her mother, or father, or somebody. I'll send the ambulance doctor back to check on her for possible injuries. Find out what you can from her. And tell the detective-sergeant to 'phone Dr. Carruthers and have him come over to the fire right away . . . And I'll want some men, quickly as possible.'

'Right, sir.'

All the time Denning had been edging urgently towards the outer doorway. In the background, from the office, he could hear Grant contacting the fire station and hospital.

Then he was out in the High Street and running towards the assembled crowd which had gathered round a towering mountain of smoke and sparks.

As he reached the scene of the holocaust Denning had no illusions any more as to the fate of 'Guardian Point 3'. It was a total ruin.

He elbowed his way through the excited crowd. His uniform gave him clearance and in the centre of the mob he came upon the outstretched figure of the florist.

Somebody with knowledge of first-aid had laid him flat on the pavement, his head against the gutter edge, and a rolled-up coat for a pillow. Thick handkerchiefs tied roughly round the upper part of his face hid, and to a certain extent assuaged, what must have been the searing pain of his burns.

Altogether, Cornelius Bedford was in a sorry state, his clothes torn and scorched, his hands skinned from the razor-edges of flames.

'Pretty bad, Inspector,' said the coatless man who had evidently done the first-aid. 'I didn't move him much in case of internal injuries.'

'You did well,' Denning muttered, bending on one knee beside the florist. 'Mr. Bedford, can you hear me?' he asked.

The bandaged head stirred slightly.

'I'm the police . . . Can you tell me anything?'

'Pay . . . Paper,' the florist whispered, and Denning bent further to catch the muffled words. 'P-pink toffee paper . . . blew up . . . on the cactus — ' The voice stopped.

As no further words came, Denning grasped the florist's shoulder and very gently shook him. There was no sign of response, and a brief testing of the man s pulse revealed that he was dead.

Denning got to his feet, his face grim, the crowd watching him — then there was a sudden stirring as the first of the fire-engines, its bell clanging, came hurtling down the High Street.

Denning stood aside and gave the firemen free passage, confining his attention to directing the three constables who had now arrived. The crowd was held back with difficulty as the ambulance arrived and the dead florist was lifted into it.

'Looks as though I've had a trip for nothing, Denning,' Dr. Preston commented.

'No fault of yours. But before that body's taken away there's something I want to find out — '

Denning climbed into the back of the ambulance, the doctor behind him, and the doors were closed, but on Denning's order through the driver's partition the ambulance did not start moving immediately.

Denning began an examination of Bedford's pockets, removing the various articles he found there. They comprised a wallet, a handkerchief, a little ball of straw, a pamphlet about seedlings, and lastly an unopened envelope with the address arranged in letters cut from a newspaper.

'I thought as much,' Denning muttered, pocketing the articles. 'Not a word to anybody about this, Doctor. I'll get out again; I'm expecting somebody to come along and examine this fire . . . Oh, by the way, Preston, there's a youngster at the police station you might have a look at on your way past. Says her eyes are troubling her. She was mixed up in the explosion. Give her a look-over, will you?'

'Pleasure,' Preston assented, and with a nod of thanks Denning climbed out of the ambulance. He slammed the doors shut and watched the ambulance move away.

A second fire-engine came clanging into view and knowing there was nothing more he could do Denning turned away — and bumped into Dr. Carruthers, homberg on the back of his head and his coat flowing open.

'I came as soon as I got the message,' he said, glancing at the slowly subduing blaze. 'But I'll have to wait for the ashes to cool before I can start looking around.'

'I didn't think of that,' Denning muttered. 'But maybe I have some information which will guide you. Just before he died, Bedford said something to me about pink toffee paper on the cactus that blew up. Probably he was raving . . . On the other hand there is a schoolgirl at the station this very moment who saw the explosion. She particularly mentioned a vivid purple flash.'

'That's interesting! I'd better talk to her.'

'All on your own this time?' Denning questioned, as Carruthers followed him down the street.

The little scientist glanced up in the fading light. 'Gordon went out — to keep a date with Miss Lloyd. He's entitled to go where he pleases after five if we've nothing special on hand . . . '

As they reached the police station Denning found that Dr. Preston had called in and gone again. The child concerned was seated on the bench opposite the enquiry counter with an immense-bosomed woman sitting solidly beside her.

'This is a nice to-do, I must say!' the large woman exclaimed as Denning and Carruthers came in. You don't think my Ethel set fire to that flower shop, do you?'

'Hardly, madam,' Denning said, with a faint smile. 'You will be her mother?'

'I am that. Mrs. Barlow's the name. And now you've come, let me tell you the doctor's 'ad a look at 'er and she's all right. So I'm taking 'er 'ome, fire or no fire.'

'Before you do that, Mrs. Barlow, the child may be able to help us,' Carruthers remarked, and for all his smallness there was something so peculiarly impressive about him that the woman did not argue the fact. She waited, wondering, as Carruthers looked down at the nervously glancing child.

'What I want you to do, young lady, is tell me exactly what happened,' he said, grinning encouragement at her.

'Yes, sir,' the girl said, speaking in her small voice as though reciting lines in a school play. 'I was just going past that flower shop — on my way 'ome from school. I was a bit late because I'd been playing with Minnie Allsop, y'see . . . Then there was an awful bang and I was thrown in the road. All I saw was a big, lovely purple flame and it hurt my eyes something awful . . . Then when I got up I saw that the shop was on fire and that poor man was lying in the gutter.'

'Purple flame,' Carruthers repeated, musing. 'Are you certain that it was *really purple*?'

'Well, no,' little Ethel confessed finally, colouring. 'It was more of a very dark blue — like — like the colour of a violet!' she added excitedly, suddenly remembering her botany lesson that afternoon.

'Ah, a violet!' Carruthers nodded, a gleam in his eyes. 'Good . . . That's all I needed to know.'

'I've a question I'd like to ask you, Ethel,' Denning said, as the child and her mother rose. 'Did you see Mr. Bedford — the florist — before the explosion?'

'Oh yes. He was messing about with his prickly plants.'

Denning nodded. 'I know what you mean. The cactus plants he had in the doorway entrance for show . . . All right, thanks — you can go now.'

''Bout time too,' observed the large woman disgustedly. 'What my Joe'll say when 'is tea isn't ready I don't know! Come on, Ethel, an' mind you don't rip them stockings no more!'

Denning turned and looked at the thoughtful Carruthers as the pair went out. The little scientist jerked his head towards the superintendent's private office, and, after telling Grant that he had better come too, Denning followed him in.

Carruthers began to pace about with his hands deep in his topcoat pockets.

'Pink toffee paper on the cactus and a violet-coloured flame,' he said, thinking. 'And I understand that these cactus plants were always outside?'

'Always,' Denning confirmed, sitting before his desk. 'I've seen them many a time. There were three of them, fairly big, in a wire-stand affair.'

'Shielded from the wind?'

Denning looked surprised. 'Shielded from the east winds which we are having at present, anyway. If they got any at all it would be from the south and south-west.'

'But no wind today,' Carruthers said. 'That's important — and the assassin, fireraiser, or what-ever you like to call him, knew it. A wind, or the lightest of touches, could have started the whole thing off prematurely. He obviously knew that and picked a good day for it — perhaps thanks to weather forecasts — just as he picked a good day for the frozen nitro-glycerin.'

'But,' Denning was not interested in these by-paths, 'what *happened*?'

Carruthers lighted a cigarette and regarded the superintendent placidly.

'What *actually* happened, I'll never be able to say. All traces will long since have disappeared. What I want you to do is come back with me to my laboratory and I'll give you what I think is the answer. Before we do that, though, I want to ask something. Why the devil didn't you take the precaution of examining that place beforehand?'

'No opportunity. The thing happened without warning — or almost. In a talk I had with the Borough Surveyor I heard enough to convince me that I ought to keep an eye on Bedford's, but before I could do a thing the place went up in smoke.'

'Mmmm . . . No advance note this time, then?'

Denning emptied his pockets of Bedford's few belongings and handed over the unopened printed envelope. Carruthers took it and read. Then he handed it back, one eyebrow raised.

'Today!' Denning exclaimed, staring at it. 'Immediately! Not tomorrow — as it said in the other notes . . . But I didn't know a thing about it. Presumably delivered today. Bedford was well known about here as a pretty absentminded old cuss — and that cost him his life. Had he come to me with this I'd have kept him out of the place at all costs.'

'I'm only interested in the scientific angles to a problem,' Carruthers murmured, 'but I would suggest that the note stipulated today because the whole attack rested on the weather remaining comparatively windless. This morning's weather forecast said rising winds for tomorrow, which might have ruined the experiment. Our attacking foe judged from yesterday's forecast that today would be suitable — but not after today. So he posted the warning.'

'He couldn't have known that Bedford wouldn't reveal the note,' Denning said. 'How would it have affected his plans if we had had the place guarded and examined?'

'You could have posted policemen all round it, but you would have had your men at a distance, a fact on which the attacker counted. At a distance, the attacker's moves would have seemed entirely natural. He would have looked interestedly at the cacti in the doorway, fingered them maybe, and then gone on his way. Nothing wrong in that . . . apparently.'

'What if I had closed the place up and forbidden Bedford to go into it?'

'You hadn't the authority to do that. You could have *asked* him to keep away from his business, but since it might have meant loss of business I'm inclined to think that he would have refused. The attacker was relying on the fact that, even if guarded, the place would still be open for business. It all relied, I think, on that moment when Bedford started to move the cacti-stand into the shop at closing time. Naturally our attacker would have found another way had he been balked. He had to destroy the shop, of course, as the third point in the property triangle.'

Denning stared. 'How do you know about that? All I said was I'd been to see the Borough Surveyor.'

'I know.' Carruthers grinned. 'Don't worry, son; it's just that I have a habit of working things out for myself. I suppose you know who's at the back of this lot?'

'I think I do — but I have to get the final proof.'

'Then we'll check our opinions later. Meantime you come with me and we'll see what we can do in the lab. That is, after we've had some tea.'

Carruthers got to his feet and as Denning did likewise he looked across at Grant who had been listening silently to the conversation.

'You'd better get through to Colonel Barrow while I'm gone, Grant, and tell him how we're getting along.'

14

Gordon Drew met Janice Lloyd at five-fifteen that evening, at the pre-arranged spot of the bus stop for Werton.

Since they went out to this busier town for tea in a café they were not aware of the fatal fire at Cornelius Bedford's . . . until the waitress brought them the cakes after the poached eggs on toast and let the news slip at the same time.

She gave them every detail, having obtained the story from a bus driver who had come from Halingford and was now off duty and having a mug of tea at the counter.

'Why,' Janice said slowly, stirring her tea mechanically, 'do these horrible things keep happening in Halingford, Gordon? Surely you've some idea, working beside Dr. Carruthers as you do?'

'I don't know what's behind it,' Gordon answered, 'even though I have seen a scientific demonstration showing how poor old Bilkin got the works.' Then at the girl's eager glance he added seriously: 'I'm afraid it's confidential. Everything Dr. Carruthers does is that, and I can't break his confidence.'

The girl hesitated, then: 'Perhaps you can tell me something else, Gordon . . . Does the business involve Father?'

'Why on earth should it?' Gordon was surprised. 'You don't think that your father's mixed up in this horrible business, surely?'

'I'm afraid,' Janice said moodily, putting a cake on her plate, 'he might be. I've told you and Dr. Carruthers about Dad being terribly worried over these disasters, haven't I? Well, why *should* he be? I'm willing to bet he'll be in an awful state tonight when he hears of this new tragedy and the death of poor old Mr. Bedford into the bargain.'

'Listen, Jan, if you think there is something the police should know you should tell them — even if it goes against your own father. If the police thought you'd withheld vital information you might get into serious trouble.'

'I know.' She rubbed her left eyebrow pensively. 'But I've nothing definite to go on — only what you might call intangible little things, because I know Father's every mood. But there's one thing that I think you should know. I found out recently that we're nearly broke.'

'No disgrace in that,' Gordon grinned. 'Except for the few pounds I have by me and the salary I get from Carruthers I'm in the same boat — '

'But with Dad it's different,' the girl broke in. 'He hasn't said anything, but I can tell by the things he denies himself — and Mother, and me. Hints and chance remarks have enabled me to build up a pretty clear picture. I think Dad has been speculating heavily and has lost practically everything through it. That, I think, is the *real* reason why he's so worried — and knowing his worry must be obvious he blames it on the disasters . . . '

'Why tell me this now, Jan?' Gordon asked.

'When you came into town on Monday I could hardly start off with a tale of woe, could I? Besides, I thought you were leaving again for London, so if you thought my fortunes were all right I saw no reason to disabuse your mind. But now we've picked up our friendship where it left off, it's only right you should know. I'm afraid it isn't a girl in a particularly high niche whom you've picked.'

Gordon patted her hand across the table. 'Janice Lloyd in *any* social position will do nicely for me. And look at what sort of a sample you are getting in me!'

'I'll take that chance. There's only one thing I'm wondering about — From where did you get that awful scar on your face? It's from — a fire, isn't it?'

'Yes,' Gordon assented quietly. 'It's from a fire, which I tried to prevent. Both Dr. Carruthers and Superintendent Denning know how I came by it, so you might as well also . . . ' And in detail he told the girl the exact same story he had related to Superintendent Denning.

'That makes me feel so much better,' she said earnestly. 'Though of course I should have known that you — ' She stopped and stared fixedly at the broad window of the café. 'Look!' she gasped, pointing.

Gordon twirled round and gazed, but only beheld passers-by in the lights from the café window and the street. He swung back to the girl who was gathering up her handbag hastily and urging him to hurry.

'Why? For what?' he demanded, scrambling out of his chair in bewilderment.

'It was Ross — that dispenser from Granwell's! I'd know him anywhere. He looked right in on us for a moment!'

* * *

It was seven o'clock when Gordon Drew reached Dr. Carruthers' home, and on being told by the housekeeper that the scientist was in the laboratory with Superintendent Denning he hurried down to find him. The little scientist propounding something didactically — then at the sight of Gordon he broke off in surprise,

'What brings you here, Gordon? Tired of the charms of Miss Lloyd so soon?'

'It isn't that, Doctor. 'Evening, Superintendent. I dashed here from Werton to tell you that Janice has seen Ross.'

'Eh?' Denning was instantly alert. 'Where?'

'In Werton. She only had a glimpse through a café window but she knows him by sight. I'd have been here sooner only the bus got a puncture. We left the café right away but couldn't trace him. I thought I'd better tell you personally. Jan and I are meeting again tomorrow night to make up for our lost date.'

'Miss Lloyd might have been mistaken,' Denning said, his eagerness evaporating. 'A glimpse through a window and in artificial light isn't much to go by. Surely Ross wouldn't be such an idiot as to walk down the main street with the police on the watch for him, of which fact he should be aware from the papers. However,' he added, 'I'll advise both Werton police and my own headquarters to be on the alert. Can I use your 'phone, Doctor?'

'Surely. Extension's over there in the corner.'

Denning went to it and gave his instructions. As he returned Gordon Drew said: 'I suppose you know about the florist's shop?'

'Know!' Carruthers hooted. 'I'm just going to demonstrate how it was done. To resume, Superintendent,' he went on, picking up the conversation at the point where Gordon had interrupted it, 'I think we are about ready.'

He went over to the distant bench by the wall and contemplated an oblong strip of pink paper, Nodding to himself he walked back the few yards to where Denning and Gordon were standing.

'Now,' he said, 'watch! I'm going to toss this ball of paper' — he picked up one which he had made, from the table beside him — 'and throw it. It's extremely light, but observe the effect.'

The ball sailed through the air and landed flush on top of the pink paper, Immediately there was a sharp report and momentary flame of the most magnificent heliotrope colour, masked slightly by a belch of smoke. The men blinked, feeling very much as though they had just witnessed a violet-tinted magnesium flash.

'Well,' Denning said admiringly, 'that seems to tally on a small scale with what that child Ethel saw. The violet colour was there all right. What is it — or was it?'

'An infinitesimal amount of iodide of nitrogen. Basically it is a mixture of several substances. You precipitate it by adding solution of iodine to ammonia and drying it on filter paper — '

'The pink toffee paper!' Denning put in quickly.

'Yes — but filter paper is only blotting paper, so don't lose any sleep over that. When it has dried — by exposure to the air — it is a brownish black powder and one of the most explosive agents known to science. The slightest movement, even the touch of a feather, will explode it. The explosion creates the beautiful violet vapour of iodine, which you saw — and which Ethel saw too.'

Denning rubbed his chin. 'Damned if I know which is the smarter trick — this, or the frozen nitro-glycerin.'

'You will see now why I asked if there

was a wind blowing on the cactus,' Carruthers said. 'If there had been it would have fired the stuff prematurely once it had dried. As things stood it didn't blow up until Bedford came to move the stand. The slight vibration did it, and there being a lot of iodide of nitrogen he was knocked spinning.'

'Suppose somebody else had bumped against the stand when going into the shop?' Gordon asked.

'Iodide of nitrogen is no respecter of persons. It would naturally have exploded just the same, the prime object being to destroy the shop. It did not matter who caused it to happen. Diabolical, I grant, but there it is.'

'But — but how was it applied? Set? Arranged?' Denning demanded. 'You said that it would merely look as if the person concerned were fingering the cactus.'

'And so it would. The creator of this ingenious little trick had simply to cut up strips of blotting paper — which the uninitiated Bedford evidently took for toffee paper — and lay them in the dry soil of the cactus plants. *Dry* soil, notice

— or compost. He then poured his solution of iodine and ammonia and other chemical substances that make up the stuff on to the blotting paper strips. Only the work of maybe thirty seconds. After that — walk off. The stuff would filter and dry gradually and would look like soil lying on top of the paper. Then, once dry, the first touch and — *wallop*!'

'And it was done in the porch outside the shop,' Denning mused. 'Was there not the chance that the explosion would have dispelled itself outside and done no more damage than burn the person who started it off?'

'There was evidently enough of the iodide to smash in the already cracked windows — and the brief, high-powered combustible flame it generates, and the blazing bits that were naturally hurled in all directions, were quite sufficient to start a fire in a dry wood and plant store such as Bedford owned. Even if the fire brigade had been on the spot, ready for an instantaneous outbreak, it would not have had an easy task with an ancient building like that.'

Silence. Carruthers went over to the bench and tidied the items that had been knocked over in the experiment. At last Denning nodded grimly.

'Earlier on,' he said, looking at Carruthers as he came forward again, 'I had formed a pretty good idea of the culprit behind all this — and this business with Bedford makes me as good as sure — and I have the motive back of it.'

Carruthers shrugged. 'When you are ready to check your conclusions against mine just let me know.'

'I'll remember that,' Denning said. 'But I'm trying to finish the thing off myself.'

'It might not mean anything,' Gordon Drew put in quietly, 'but there's something you might like to know. It's about Mr. Lloyd — Janice's father. You remember she told us how worried he is over these fire disasters — '

'Well?' There was an uncompromising look on Denning's face.

'She thinks it isn't so much because of the fires, but because of lack of money. Her father is nearly on the rocks. Speculations and so forth. You know how it is with these big-shot chaps . . . '

'Yes . . . I do.' There was a curious significance in Denning's tone. 'Thanks, Mr. Drew, for the information. Now I've got to be getting back to headquarters . . . thanks again for your help, Doctor. You'll be hearing from me.'

* * *

Janice Lloyd had indeed seen Clayton Ross through the café window, but he had not seen her. His main aim, now the long distance bus had brought him from London to Werton — and to London he had travelled by bus from Birmingham — was to get out of the bright lights of the street and into the shadowy by-ways. In this he succeeded and Janice and Gordon Drew, on the lookout for him lost him utterly. Not that he was aware, of course, of how narrowly he had escaped.

Not that it would have signified: he was on his way to Halingford police station determined on only one thing — an interview with Superintendent Denning. He was so anxious indeed to bring to an end the hole-and-corner existence he had been leading for the past few days, that he had not the patience to wait for the Halingford bus, which still required another twelve minutes before it would become due.

Instead he walked along the quiet, night-ridden road that connected the two towns, resolved to catch the bus at a stop further along the route.

The night was dampish and quiet with low-banked mist lying in the meadows on either side of the hedges as he tramped along. In one hand he carried a suitcase containing enough articles for a night's stay in Halingford and no more.

What he would have to say to Denning could just as easily have been said to the Birmingham police and they in turn could have relayed it to Halingford — but this was not Clayton Ross's way.

He considered that the man who had been doing all the hard work in the investigation — Denning — was alone entitled to the exclusive information. And so, risking the alertness of the police in Birmingham, he had taken the plunge

— and probably because of the audacity of the act in broad daylight, had got clean away with it.

The chief reason was doubtless because the police — not of course concentrating solely on him by any means — had kept their sharpest watch at the railway stations and he had instead taken a long-distance bus from a stop miles from the main terminus. And now there was only a matter of a few miles between him and his goal — Halingford.

Once or twice as he tramped along he glanced back to see if the lights of the bus were approaching. They were not, as yet, and it was on the third occasion that he fancied he caught sight of a figure for a moment. Only the dimmest outlines, a faint silhouette against the glow which was cast by the lights of Werton in the background, but —

Ross came to an abrupt stop, and the action satisfied his suspicions. A second or two afterwards other footsteps came to a stop, the owner of which had obviously been caught off guard.

Ross hesitated, on the verge of calling

out — then he checked himself. It might be a member of the police force following him. It might be . . . anything, he decided, and not of particularly good omen either.

He went on again, his lips tight and his ears alert for the least sound behind him.

This time, the pursuer never allowed his footsteps to over-run those of Ross as he stopped now and again — and though he kept on glancing behind him Ross saw no sign of the pursuer nor, to his increasing consternation, any sign of the bus. Had he but known it the bus in question was having its front wheel changed in Werton Square at that very moment, its tyre deflated from a puncture.

For another mile the cat-and-mouse business went on, and by this time the glow that came from Halingford was commencing to appear ahead. It caused the pursuer to race suddenly out of the dark with no regard any more for quietness.

Ross heard the rush of footsteps, dropped his case and clenched his fists.

He had a momentary vision of a short, powerful man with very square, broad shoulders — then a fist slammed out of the dark and took him with terrific impact under the jaw.

Ross went stumbling backwards helplessly and crashed on his back in the road. He was not a powerful man, but the consciousness of his predicament made him lash out with all his power at the man who plunged on top of him.

Ross knew in that moment that if he didn't break free from the iron grip that had suddenly seized his throat his life was forfeit.

He fought, he tore, he kicked — but the strength of the man gripping him was phenomenal. The struggling men rolled over the grass verge of the road and into the soggy wet of the ditch beyond.

Ross felt the fingers tightening into his throat — harder, and harder still, then suddenly his face was thrust violently under the surface of the muddy, brackish water. His lungs, already choked for lack of air, were quite incapable of coping with this new outrage. He knew he was struggling with increasing weakness, that his senses were floating away into a world where there was no air, a tearing pain in his lungs, an unbelievable steel grip upon his windpipe . . .

⋆ ⋆ ⋆

Denning arrived back at the police station to find Detective-Sergeant Grant in his own office in the act of making an inventory of the articles taken from the pockets of the deceased Cornelius Bedford.

'Come into my office, Grant,' Denning instructed briefly, and with a nod the detective-sergeant followed him into it.

'Anything happened?' Denning asked, settling at his desk.

'I've been round to Jones to get him to sign his statement. And I rang up the Old Boy, as you asked. He was out, so I gave the report in the usual way.'

Denning gestured impatiently. 'Skip the routine: any sign of Clayton Ross?'

'Not the least, sir. And if you ask me I don't think there will be. Miss Lloyd must have been mistaken.'

'Maybe . . . '

'What happened at Dr. Carruthers', sir?' Grant asked. 'Had he worked out how the latest attack was caused?'

'He most certainly had — to the tune of iodide of nitrogen.' And the superintendent covered the facts.

'Which confirms your earlier belief, sir — that we're looking for an expert chemist. I just wonder if Miss Lloyd *did* see Ross?'

'That I don't know,' Denning said, sitting back in his chair, 'but there's one thing I *do* know: I'm beginning to get this whole damned business into its right perspective at last. The only thing I want is the final corroboration; that I've got to have before I can apply for a warrant. Now, if only we could lay our hands on Clayton Ross — !'

'Quite a few men are out looking for him, sir, as you instructed. For myself,' Grant went on, 'I have formed the opinion that — ' He broke off suddenly as the sergeant-in-charge tapped on the office door and admitted the tall, eagle-like figure of the Chief Constable.

'Good evening, Denning — glad to find you here. 'Evening, Grant. The moment I returned and got your report I came straight over.' Colonel Barrow found a seat and regarded the superintendent from under his tufted sandy eyebrows. 'Bit more dirty work by our unknown enemy of society, eh? And another life lost?'

'I'm afraid so, sir — but chiefly because I had no advance warning of what was coming. Bedford was warned like the others but he failed to let me know . . . '

'I'd like the facts,' the Old Boy said, somewhat testily. His mind was already picturing the newspapers of the following morning, which could only list another failure on the part of the Halingford police to prevent a mysterious and tragic fire.

Denning, augmenting the telephone report that Grant had already given, gave every fact that had come to light since the Colonel's last visit, including a résumé of Carruthers' experiment with iodide of nitrogen. When he had had all his questions answered the Chief Constable fixed Denning with a look.

'You said you were going to clear this thing up if I gave you your head. How far back has this fresh tragedy thrown you? Be quite frank with me. If you're getting out of your depth I must call in the Yard.'

'I'm far less out of my depth than I was, sir,' Denning replied firmly. 'I was just remarking to Grant as you arrived that I only want final corroboration of my theories from Clayton Ross before I take out a warrant.'

'Then Ross isn't the man we want?'

'As the culprit — no. The person who sent the note warning Bilkin to get out could not have planned the nitro-ice trick because it would have defeated its own purpose. Since we are more or less satisfied from the newsagent that Ross was responsible for the warning the assumption is that he got to know of what was coming and took prompt steps to try and save Bilkin without involving himself. I believe that he then left town to avoid being implicated in case of trouble. He knew trouble would descend on him once the attacker knew that Bilkin had been warned beforehand, a fact that would — and did — become obvious from the newspaper reports . . . '

Denning stopped as the telephone shrilled. 'Excuse me,' he muttered, raising the instrument. 'Yes, what is it?'

'Werton police on the line, sir,' said the sergeant's loud voice in the receiver. 'Very important . . . '

Denning aimed an expectant glance at the waiting Chief Constable. 'Perhaps they've got Ross . . . Yes, hello? Denning here. Oh, it's you, sir! Yes . . . ' Denning listened and his expression gradually changed. 'Manual strangulation, eh?' His face became grimmer and the Chief Constable and Grant exchanged quick glances. 'Yes, of course. Right away. Thanks . . . '

He put the telephone down and looked at the Colonel. 'Ross has been found, sir, but it doesn't help us much. P.C. Robinson on his patrol down the Halingford-Werton road saw a hand sticking out of the ditch. He pulled the body out and sent for the Werton police, their territory being nearer to the body than ours. The body has since been identified as that of Clayton Ross . . . Oh, blast!' the superintendent finished savagely. 'The one witness I needed! And now . . . I'm going over to Werton to see for myself,' he added, picking up his uniform cap. 'Coming with me?'

The Colonel nodded and got to his feet. They were in the police car speeding down the dark road from Halingford to Werton before the Colonel made a comment.

'You mentioned that Miss Lloyd thought she saw him in Werton tonight. Evidently she was right. What do you imagine his intentions could have been?'

'All I can think of is that Ross was heading for Halingford — which is probably right since he was seen in Werton by Miss Lloyd — and was found midway between there and Halingford — and perhaps intended to see me. Somebody was obviously aware of his movements and deliberately silenced him. What he could have told me would, I think, have blown this whole filthy plot sky-high.'

'You haven't said outright whom you believe is back of everything,' the Colonel remarked rather dryly. 'I think I am entitled to know!'

'I want to be *sure*, sir, first,' Denning said doggedly. 'It's the only safe method. There's one way, though, in which you can help me.'

'And that is?'

'Find out the exact state of the Borough Surveyor's bank account.'

'Good heavens, man, what for? I've no authority to do a thing like that — and, anyway, the manager wouldn't tell me.'

'He'll tell you if you demand to know — in an official capacity, of course. You know that, sir.'

'Oh yes, I know the law can root out the facts in a case of criminal suspicion, but . . . Dammit, Denning, you're going wrong somewhere! Lloyd is one of my closest friends!'

'Only you, as the Chief Constable, can do it, sir — and I *must* know,' Denning insisted with quiet emphasis, at which the

Colonel finally grumbled a grudging assent. He had no time to ask further questions for in another few minutes they came into Werton's main street and Denning pulled up the car outside the police station with its distinctive round opal globe.

Inspector Fanshaw of the Werton police was waiting. Formalities over, he led the way into the drab back area of the big police headquarters and finally into a back room. Upon the long, solitary deal table, a cloth thrown over him, lay Clayton Ross. Denning raised the cover and looked at the face. Then he gave a questioning glance.

'I suppose it *is* Ross?' he enquired.

'So his landlady verified,' Fanshaw said. 'She's only just left. I had her driven over to identify him — the address of his Halingford rooms was in his wallet.'

'The doc seen him yet?' Denning questioned.

'Yes, and he verified our belief of manual strangulation, which took place somewhere about six-thirty this evening. If there are any other causes of death they'll come out when he makes the postmortem later tonight. Now you've seen the body I can have it sent to the mortuary.'

'I saw some of your men working in the road as we drove here,' Denning said. 'Any sign yet of who did it?'

'Not yet,' Fanshaw said.

'Was there anything particular found on Ross outside the address of his rooms?' Denning questioned, and for answer the Inspector led the way into his own private office and pointed to an assortment of articles on his desk. The superintendent and Chief Constable walked across and studied them.

There was a handkerchief, a well-worn leather wallet, the contents of which were beside it and comprised a cutting headed 'This Week in Parliament', two snapshots of a remarkably pretty girl with blonde hair, the return half of a bus ticket for Birmingham-London and some money in notes and coins, a copy of the *Birmingham Herald* for that morning — Friday — and a bunch of keys.

'I suppose this is the lot?' Denning

asked finally, and Inspector Fanshaw nodded.

'Did you expect something more?'

'Not exactly. I just wondered if there happened to be a pair of small nail scissors with curved blades. All right, never mind. Plenty here that is useful, sir, anyway,' he added, glancing at the intent Colonel. 'For one thing our guess that he departed to Birmingham must have been right. This return bus ticket shows it. It also shows something else — that he was reasonably confident of the fact that he'd go back there.'

'Implying that he didn't consider himself guilty enough to be charged and taken in custody,' the Chief Constable agreed, thinking. 'It looks as though he was going to make a statement, after all.'

'I'm sure of it,' Denning said quietly. 'Further, these snapshots are probably of Claire Denbury, the chorus girl who'd have been helping us by now except for that appendicitis operation. Since her show is in Birmingham this week and Ross came from there it's obvious he has been in touch with her. For that reason I think I should go to Birmingham immediately and have a talk with her the moment she's able. Ross has been silenced — as Claire herself might have been, had not the hospital given her complete protection. There's a chance she may know what Ross was going to do.'

'Well . . . maybe,' Colonel Barrow said doubtfully.

'It's psychology, sir. Women — especially those in whom a man has infinite faith — can make a man do all kinds of things. I have the feeling that Ross would have stayed away from Halingford indefinitely except perhaps for Claire. Call it a hunch if you like, but I'm hoping that maybe she urged him to make a statement, a thing which he probably would not have done of his own accord knowing — as he must have done, if this *Birmingham Herald* is any guide — that the police were on the look-out for him.'

'I think you've a good idea there, Superintendent,' Fanshaw said.

'And so do I!' Colonel Barrow declared. 'Go to it Denning: do the thing in your own way. I'll take charge in your absence as far as routine matters are concerned. Beyond that I'm not going to interfere in your show because I'm confident you can finish it.'

'Thank you, sir,' Denning smiled. 'I'll just ring up Birmingham and tell the police there to call off the hunt for Clayton Ross and to leave Claire Denbury entirely to me . . . '

He picked up the telephone and spent some five minutes explaining things to Birmingham; then he rang up the Birmingham General Hospital and spoke to the matron. It did not take him long to find out that by the following afternoon the girl would be permitted to have visitors.

'That will do for me, Matron,' Denning said, 'and I'll be there.'

He put the telephone down again and thought for a moment. 'Tomorrow afternoon,' he said slowly. 'Saturday . . . Yes, I can just manage it.'

'Manage it?' the Chief Constable exclaimed in surprise. 'You can reach Birmingham in a couple of hours, surely?'

'Yes sir, I know, but I've two special

calls to make in London first — before noon. One is at Somerset House, where I want to look through the birth records, and the other is at the Allied and Industrial Insurance Trust. I've reason to think I can get a lot of information out of both. I should be able to polish that off by eleven o'clock, then I can carry straight on to Birmingham and have lunch on the train. I'll go to London overnight and be ready to start there first thing in the morning.'

'Good enough,' the Chief Constable agreed.

'And, sir,' Denning added, 'it's unlikely that I'll be delayed very long in Birmingham, but if I am and the inquests on Ross and Bedford come up I'll leave it to you to secure an adjournment, as in the case of Bilkin . . . One other thing, suppress all information from the media about Bedford and Ross, that is, as much as possible. I may be able to get more out of Claire Denbury if she doesn't know Ross is dead.'

15

Arriving in London in the early hours of Saturday morning, having slept in the train, Denning — in plain clothes and carrying a suitcase — waited until seven o'clock in the station waiting room.

Then he had breakfast, shaved, and at the stroke of nine entered the mighty building of the Allied and Industrial Insurance Trust. Here he patiently awaited the arrival of the general manager.

This thin-nosed, flawlessly dressed, arithmetical personage arrived at ten o'clock and Denning was closeted with him in the private office for forty-five minutes. When he left the building at quarter to eleven the superintendent was smiling to himself.

A taxi whirled him to the Strand and Somerset House in record time, but it took him another hour to find the particular entry in the records for which he was searching.

For about the first time in this involved case he had discovered a straight, clear lead — and he brooded over it as a taxi whirled him to the station and the first available train to Birmingham — 12.10.

He had lunch on the train and then spent the rest of the trip jotting down various observations in his pocketbook, tying up several points and slowly but inevitably creating a logical pattern that gave the answer to the whole sinister scheme which had blasted Halingford wide open . . .

He reached Birmingham, and then the General Hospital by ten to three. Once he had made himself known he was quickly directed down spotless corridors to the women's ward, where a nurse indicated Claire Denbury lying in bed reading. She glanced round as she saw Denning approaching and lowered her magazine to the coverlet.

'Good afternoon, Miss Denbury,' Denning murmured, smiling as he removed his hat. 'I'm glad to learn that you're sufficiently recovered to see me.'

In spite of the ordeal from which she was only just recovering she looked strikingly pretty. Her face was oval, with straight, regular features and a pleasing mouth. The eyes were blue-grey, entirely frank, and the hair thick and blonde. Even dressed in the unbecoming hospital gown Denning had no difficulty in picturing that she must be an asset to any chorus troupe.

'You'll be Superintendent Denning of Halingford?' She kept her voice low so the half-dozing occupant of the next bed would not hear her. 'I was told that you would be coming to see me.'

'That's right . . . ' Denning drew up a chair and sat close to her so they could converse in whispers.

'The Birmingham police have also been trying to get into touch with me,' she said. 'Naturally, in the state I was in it was impossible. Will they be back?'

'No they won't, Miss Denbury. I'm in charge now.'

The girl's blue-grey eyes gave him a perfectly steady look and he found himself noticing how long her lashes were. Being only thirty-eight the superintendent could be forgiven for finding this particular task much more pleasurable than businesslike.

'Er . . . ' Denning considered for a moment. 'You are, of course, a very intimate friend of Mr. Clayton Ross?'

She smiled faintly. 'Of course I am. We're going to be married — when his position improves. You don't have to beat round the bush in regard to Clay, Superintendent. I know just why you're here. It's to find out if everything he told you is true, isn't it?'

'I'm afraid not, Miss Denbury,' Denning said quietly: 'I'm afraid I have bad news for you. Mr. Ross was murdered last night, at a spot between Halingford and Werton. Since you have said he was going to tell me something, which fact I had already conjectured, I might as well add that I know nothing. He never reached me.'

'Clay . . . is . . . *dead*?' Claire Denbury could hardly get the words out, then as Denning nodded he saw her eyes suddenly mist with tears and for quite three minutes he could only sit watching her, feeling decidedly embarrassed as the girl buried her face in the pillow and wept.

'I — I hate myself for being so brutal,' he said awkwardly. 'It had to be done, though, and that's why I'm here. We found out that you were his fiancée and it occurred to me that you might probably know of his intentions — '

'Of course I knew!' she interrupted, dabbing at her lashes. 'He left Halingford and came straight to find me when he first realized what was going on in that town. I arranged for a quiet place where he could stay. At first I didn't know what it was all about, then I read in the papers that the police were after him. When he first arrived in town he simply said he had left his job and was going to look for work in Birmingham here. But when I realized he was suspected of arson and murder I had to get at the truth. I made him tell me everything.'

'Go on,' Denning said gently.

'He gave me the facts, as he swore they had occurred. I told him that it was his duty to go back to Halingford immediately and tell all he knew. But he was afraid to. He said he might be murdered if he did — and that the police might not believe his story anyway, and arrest him. He had no proof, you see . . . '

The girl's slender hands had begun working fiercely at the edge of the coverlet as she looked at Denning fixedly.

'Then came that second fire, at Mr. Granwell's emporium. I insisted to Clay that he must go back, that that sort of thing might just go on if he didn't speak. After that I couldn't plead with him any more because I was suddenly taken ill and rushed to this hospital. The first thing I found, when I could begin to take interest in things again, was a letter from Clay saying that he had decided in view of a third fire to risk everything and go back to Halingford. That he wouldn't be away for . . . long.' The girl's voice broke as she fought back tears.

'I'd like to see that note, if I may,' Denning said quietly.

She nodded and he handed her the small handbag from the bedside table as she motioned to it. From it she took the letter and gave it to him. He read, his face thoughtful:

'Dearest Claire,

Thinking things over I realize now that things may only go from bad to worse if I continue to remain silent. Though I still feel that I am taking a frightful risk in going back into the 'lion's den' I am now prepared to do it as the right and honourable thing to do.

I hope and pray that you will recover from your operation and be well on the road to health when I return. You may be sure I shall not stay away a moment longer than is necessary. Should you have recovered sufficiently to move on with the company to another town leave your forwarding address as usual.

Ever yours,

Clay.'

'This, in itself, is complete vindication of Mr. Ross, Miss Denbury,' Denning said, handing the letter back. 'It's sad that the vindication has to be posthumous.'

'Clay never did a wrong thing in his life!' the girl declared. 'All he did was get himself in a mess through trying to protect other people. He talked a lot, of course — always wanting to change the world — but I liked him for it. I — I understood him so well.'

'I'm afraid,' Denning said, 'I shall have to insist on your being more explicit. What exactly did he tell you?'

'Well, it seemed that he was dissatisfied with his quarters in the dispensary at the emporium. Whilst he knew because of some legal clause there wasn't much chance of the quarters being improved, he did think he could talk Mr. Granwell into taking a lot of cumbersome stock out of the way and so make for more room. That was last Monday evening. He chose five-thirty to go up and see Mr. Granwell about it, but when he got to the office he paused for a moment before knocking on the door. In that moment he distinctly heard somebody saying 'there's no other way to do the thing except by destroying Bilkin's shop the morning after tomorrow. It'll take that long to fix things'. He got such a shock that he was afraid he might be caught and so dashed back to the dispensary. That's the gist as far as I can remember it.'

'And arrived back in the dispensary 'looking like a ghost', as his assistant put it,' Denning mused. 'And whose voice did he overhear? Granwell's?'

'No, it wasn't Mr. Granwell's. It was a voice he had never heard before. He said it sounded to him as though the speaker were half protesting.'

'And then?' Denning prompted.

'Poor Clay was in a quandary. He didn't want to reveal that he had heard anything, yet he felt that the Bilkin family might be in danger — so he hit on the idea of sending a warning, clipping it out of newspapers, he said. He reasoned that Bilkin might take heed and make himself safe. On the other hand, if nothing at all happened at the Bilkin shop after all it would be assumed that the warning had been a hoax and nobody would know who sent it. So he sent off the warning. But after he had sent it he became uneasy again. Suppose something did happen? Would the police manage to trace the note afterwards and blame him for the crime? And also, when the real criminal knew that Bilkin had been warned beforehand, as he would through the newspapers of course, he would also know that somebody knew his plans.

'Clay reasoned that if it was found out that he — Clay — had sent the warning his life wouldn't be worth anything. Anybody who could be ruthless enough to destroy the Bilkin place without warning wouldn't hesitate to kill him before he could say too much. So, he left town early on the morning the business was due to happen, staying overnight in Werton after leaving his Halingford rooms, and then came on to Birmingham to find me.'

'I take it,' Denning said finally, 'that you were too ill to read the report on the second fire, which destroyed Granwell's?'

'The full report, yes. All I've seen are past references to it.'

'In which case you don't know that warning was sent to Granwell as well, posted in Halingford the same as Bilkin's was.'

'Then — who sent it?' Claire asked

blankly. 'It couldn't have been Clay. He stayed in Birmingham from the day he arrived until yesterday afternoon, when he started back for Halingford.'

'There was even a third warning to the florist,' Denning said seriously. 'But I am quite prepared to believe that Mr. Ross didn't send them. I believe all you have told me, Miss Denbury, because it fits in almost exactly with my own conclusions. The pity is that Mr. Ross didn't take the police into his confidence and tell us what he had overheard. He would be alive now, and these disasters could doubtless have been stopped. However, I realize his dilemma: he had no proof, and for that reason didn't have the courage to speak. A great pity.'

There was a long silence, then the girl stirred a little and gave a deep sigh.

'All I want just now is for whoever murdered poor Clay to be found and punished! I'm not a vicious, spiteful sort of girl, but to kill poor Clay just because he tried to help is to me the most horrible injustice ever. You will find out who did it, Superintendent, won't you?'

'I know who did it,' he answered, and her eyes widened. 'I've known for some time — but in my business I have to be careful. There is a matter of proof to always be satisfied. You have my assurance that this whole affair will be cleared up and your late fiancé's murderer brought to trial.' Denning got to his feet, hesitating over a matter that had now become personal instead of professional.

'You will of course be called as a witness at the trial,' he said, reflecting, 'And that will be a somewhat harrowing business for you.'

'I'll — manage,' the girl said, hesitating, and looked as though she were trying to read Denning's mind.

'It's much easier when you have a little coaching beforehand,' he explained, clearing his throat gently. 'Courts are not really terrifying places when you know the ropes . . . as I do. I was wondering if . . . I — er — I suppose you have to join the company again as soon as you are better?'

Claire gave that serious little smile of hers.

'Not that quickly, Superintendent, and I'm not that terribly important, you know. Besides, we have a union to protect us. I'm on at least three weeks' sick leave, which will give me ample time to recover. As a chorus girl I'll need that long to recover. I'm even wondering if I'll choose something less strenuous . . . '

'I was just thinking . . . If you would care to come to Halingford when you're fit to travel I could soon put you in the way of all that will be required of you at the trial. It's country round Halingford, you know. Build you up. The Grand Hotel is quite a decent place to stay.'

'It's nice of you to want to make things so easy for me,' Claire said, her blue-grey eyes regarding him curiously.

'After what's happened you're entitled to it, Miss Denbury. Just think it over, and if you decide to come let me know — Superintendent Denning, Halingford Police Department, Halingford.' He passed her a card. 'This also gives my phone number if you decide to 'phone . . . Now I really must be going, and I'm sorry I had to bring you such bad news.'

He grasped her hand and shook it gently, deciding again that those eyelashes of hers were amazingly beautiful.

'Goodbye, Superintendent,' she responded. 'For the time being.'

Denning left the bedside, his back straighter than usual as he went down the ward. He realized that the girl would be watching him out of sight. It was only with great difficulty that he kept his mind fixed on the essentials of the situation and what he had learned.

He wondered whether the seed he had planted would germinate. It had to him suddenly become a matter of uncommon importance whether Miss Claire Denbury would come to Halingford . . . or not.

⋆ ⋆ ⋆

During Denning's absence the Halingford and Werton police, working together, had not been idle either.

Though the marks of the scuffling feet in the light, stony gravel-surfacing of the Werton-Halingford road told them nothing definite, there was an abrupt turn for the better when Clayton Ross's abandoned suitcase was found, flung in a ditch about half a mile away from where his body had been discovered. This the police found at breakfast time when, in London, Denning had been setting off for the Allied and Industrial Insurance Trust.

Since, according to Janice Lloyd, Ross had been seen going from Werton in the direction of Halingford, and had been strangled before completing his journey, it seemed to Inspector Fanshaw and the Chief Constable that the suitcase had been thrown away by the murderer, and not by Ross himself, it being found nearer Halingford than Werton.

Immediately every available source of enquiry, and particularly the drivers on the bus route, was investigated. By noon, Detective Sergeant Jackson of the Werton police had obtained definite results.

The driver on Route 17 the previous night — whose bus had developed the puncture — had observed a powerful, short, square-shouldered man going along the lane, had seen him clearly in the light of the headlamps for a moment, and it had seemed to the driver as though the man had been caught by surprise by the bus's approach, for he had jumped to one side of the lane. He had been carrying a suit-case.

With this knowledge in their possession — and also the facts of the Bilkin affair which had stated that the ice-man had the same description — the combined police forces moved fast in their endeavours to trace the man. In trying to find him locally they were unsuccessful, and it was actually owing to Denning's own efforts that they finally located their quarry.

Denning had already issued a description of him to all stations in order that he might be brought for an interview. An alert constable in Barchester, twenty miles away, observed a man of this identical description hanging round a bus stop at four o'clock in the afternoon, questioned him, and then accompanied him to the nearest police-station.

Superintendent Denning, returning to Halingford towards eight in the evening, was greeted with the pleasant discovery that 'square shoulders' was in custody, having so far refused to answer any of the questions put to him.

'It's good hearing anyway, sir,' Denning remarked to the Chief Constable. 'How did you get him so quickly?'

The Colonel briefly outlined the events.

'We might have chased the man for weeks but for his description being out,' he explained. 'I had him brought here instead of Werton. This business is in your territory, after all. We can't get anything out of him, but maybe you can.'

'I can try,' Denning said, putting down his suitcase in a corner of the office. 'And the sooner the better, then he can be moved to Werton prior to appearing before the magistrates.'

Denning nodded to Grant who was standing awaiting instructions, and the detective-sergeant left the office.

'Did you see that girl Claire Denbury?' the Chief Constable asked.

'I did, sir, and learned all I wanted . . . Tell you about it afterwards.'

Denning pulled off his hat and overcoat, then sat down at the desk and waited until 'square shoulders' was ushered in from the detention-room at the back of the station, Grant behind him.

In the light the man was revealed as immensely strong in physique, though short. His face was square and reminiscent of a boxer's, with slightly flattened nose and audacious blue eyes. Thick dark hair grew low down on his forehead. What neck he possessed was almost non-existent. Denning summed him up silently and then lowered his gaze to the hands. They were large and coarse with a purple-red skin.

Denning picked up the official report from where it had been placed. It stated briefly that 'square shoulders' — otherwise giving his name as Harry Raycliff — did 'feloniously, wilfully and of his malice aforethought, kill and murder Clayton Ross against the peace of our Sovereign, the Queen, Her Crown and Dignity'.

'You are Harry Raycliff?' Denning asked curtly, glancing up.

'Good a name as any, isn't it?' the man asked truculently.

'Have it your own way. The name

doesn't signify: we'll find your right one if we have to. You've no need to make a statement without legal advice if you don't wish — '

'I'm not saying anything to anybody,' the man snapped. 'But I'll tell you one thing: you'll never pin the murdering of Clayton Ross, or whatever his name was, on me. You've not got a thing to go on.'

'I haven't had time yet to examine the evidence in that regard,' Denning answered. 'I'm chiefly interested in other matters — especially the ice-block you delivered to Mr. Bilkin on the day his shop was blown to pieces. What have you to say about that?'

'Nothing! I don't know what you're talking about.'

'Oh yes, you do, my friend! You bribed one Bill Higgins of the Cold Ice Company to lend you his ice-truck on the morning Bilkin had his ice delivery. You then returned the truck to Werton after delivering the ice to Bilkin. Where did you get that ice? Who gave it to you?'

'I'm not sayin' anythin', and you can't make me!'

'True,' Denning replied, 'but I think you might like to know that it wasn't ice you delivered but frozen nitro-glycerin. Had you made one error, gone over one extra heavy bump with that truck, you would have been blown to pieces! Whoever gave you the ice knew it, and risked it. In plain language, you were played for a sucker. You could easily have been killed!'

Raycliff's expression changed as malevolent fury crossed his blunt features.

'Why, the dirty — ' He checked himself and gave a cynical grin. 'But I wasn't. And I'm not sayin' anythin'.'

'Why not make things easier for yourself?' Denning asked shrewdly. 'I'm prepared to believe that you murdered Clayton Ross on express instructions from somebody else, and not of your own initiative. But if you persist in 'saying nothing' you'll get the full brunt of the responsibility.'

It was Denning's last card, and it failed. The round head with the low-growing hair shook stubbornly. 'You're wasting your time, Superintendent. I've nothing to say.'

'Why,' Denning demanded, losing his temper, 'are you such an idiot? What's it worth to you to hide somebody who didn't care whether you died or not? Don't you realize what sort of a spot you're in?'

Harry Raycliff remained silent. Denning motioned with his hand. With the detective-sergeant accompanying him Raycliff was led out of the office.

'No go,' the Chief Constable sighed. 'He's either stupid or very deep: hanged if I know which.'

'Probably deep,' Denning growled. 'He's perhaps banking on the fact that he may be acquitted, as indeed he may — lack of motive, and so on; and if he were acquitted and had named somebody else as his instigator that person would make sure of paying his account. With Raycliff, I think, silence is the best way of preserving his future.'

'Mmmm — possibly,' the Chief Constable agreed. 'Anyway, what else have we got? How much did you get out of your Birmingham trip?'

'I saw Miss Denbury — and a

remarkably attractive girl she is too. I got all the necessary facts concerning Clayton Ross . . . ' And Denning gave them in detail whilst the Colonel listened without interrupting.

'Then,' the Chief Constable said finally, 'that lets him out entirely, as far as the fires are concerned, anyway. But who sent the other two warnings after Ross had gone?'

'That, sir, isn't so difficult to follow when you've followed the case as I have,' Denning answered. 'First, though, I've a question to ask you. Did you make enquiry of Mr. Lloyd's bank?'

'I did, yes — and I confess I nearly overlooked it in the effort to find our square-shouldered friend. However — Lloyd is pretty nearly on the rocks.'

Denning's eyes gleamed. 'That's exactly what I thought. That being so I think this business is about cleaned up, sir. And here's how I work it out . . . '

Detective-Sergeant Grant came back into the office and with a glance at him Denning added: 'You'd better hear what I have to say, Grant. This whole scheme, as is evidenced by the destruction of three principal buildings in the town centre is the work of a ruthless commercialist to extend his power and gain a complete monopoly, by degrees, over the entire town. That man is, of course, Rupert Granwell.'

16

The Chief Constable stirred a little. 'Granwell! I thought you said the Borough Surveyor — '

'No, sir, I didn't say that. I merely said I wanted to know the state of Mr. Lloyd's finances. As I see it Mr. Lloyd is hopelessly involved with Granwell and can't help himself. A man who is desperately short of money hardly can.'

'You mean to tell me that Granwell burned down his own place!' the Colonel exclaimed.

'I do — for a double reason; but I'll come to that in its proper time. Let me take the events in order. First, Granwell is a councillor, and we know full well from reports on Council debates that he has tried for a long time to get the Council to find some way of abrogating the clause which makes Halingford Road incapable of alteration, that is, as long as three points of it, occupied originally by Bilkin, Granwell's immediate neighbour, and Bedford, remained standing.

'Perhaps when Granwell first came to Halingford he didn't know about that clause: he only became a councillor after the erection of his emporium. But once in the Council secrets he would soon find out that he could never extend his business with those three points remaining to legally block him — so he hit on the idea of wiping them out. He must have found out that the Borough Surveyor was financially embarrassed — there were dozens of ways he could discover that — and he also knew that the Borough Surveyor would suspect the accidents were not natural when they happened to those three points in particular. So, I think, Lloyd connived with him.'

'I'd never thought Lloyd was that kind of a man,' the Colonel muttered,

'I don't think he is, really. I believe Granwell — as the price of the Borough Surveyor keeping quiet — offered him some alluring prospect on the Council when the matter was finished and Granwell had bought up all the land hereabouts and erected his own various stores upon it. It would, by sheer force, make Granwell the most powerful councillor and probably the next mayor. He could hire and fire at will. I'll warrant that Lloyd was prepared to collude with him rather than see ahead of him the prospect of losing his job if he failed to comply — and maybe even arrest for complicity. Hence his present intense worry because he knows now that murder has been added to arson, a thing he probably never bargained for.'

'How did Ross fit into it?' the Colonel asked.

'I have told you what Ross told Claire Denbury, sir. When he stopped outside Granwell's office he heard a strange voice, speaking half in protest, and referring to the fact that Bilkin's shop would be blown up the morning after the next. I believe the strange voice belonged to the Borough Surveyor, talking things over with Granwell, and by sheer chance Ross overheard part of the scheme. It was the incalculable factor, which altered everything.

'Ross used a clumsy expedient to warn Bilkin. Then, suddenly afraid of the consequences, he got out of town. *But*, when he read that Bilkin had been *warned* of what was coming, imagine Granwell's feelings! The disappearance of Ross must have convinced him that Ross had sent that warning — and not, perhaps, the Borough Surveyor, who as a mature man would never have taken such a chance. Ross was notoriously scatter-brained in some things. You observe the position in which Granwell was placed?

'Ross had established a precedent! It looked to everybody as though the attacker sent a warning before the onslaught. Granwell knew that everybody, including the police, thought that Ross was the culprit and so seized the chance to deflect blame to him. So he himself sent a warning each time before a disaster, to make matters look consistent.'

'Yes,' Colonel Barrow admitted, 'I can see that. Then that *Gazette* we found had been left by Granwell, not Ross?'

'Definitely. And it was probably the self-same *Gazette* I had seen Granwell reading in his office the previous evening. According to Dr Carruthers curved nail scissors had been used to cut out the letters for the warning. Yet there were none in the effects of Ross. Remember me asking?'

Denning paused for a moment and leafed through the various notes he had made on his way to and from Birmingham.

'Then Granwell *did* set fire to his own place?' the Chief Constable asked.

'Obviously,' Denning answered. 'When we — Dr. Carruthers, Mr. Drew, Grant and myself — went over the emporium there was no sign of anything having been arranged for a fire, but Granwell did not leave with us! He said he had some correspondence to attend to. I thought nothing of it at the time: as the owner of the place it seemed the most logical thing in the world, but later I remembered it. In that odd half-hour he arranged all the details for the fire . . .

'Further, when that evening I asked

him for the address of Stuart Jones he stolidly refused to enter the emporium to look through the files. I thought it was nervousness in case there was an explosion; but it was because the whole fire set-up would have been discovered. Where we made our mistake was in not examining the place again immediately before starting our vigil — but then, there wouldn't have been time . . .'

'And this man Raycliff?' the Chief Constable asked.

'Raycliff,' Denning answered, 'is but one of many men whom Granwell has working for him — the kind of thug who'd do anything for money. We'll find out about that from Granwell himself when we arrest him, as I intend to do without delay. It occurred to me that that frozen nitro-glycerin could not have travelled very far: the most likely place seemed to be the emporium. Remember that everything happened before the emporium staff arrived for the day's work. There was nothing to prevent Granwell staying the night in the emporium preparing the nitro-glycerin in the dispensary and letting Raycliff have it at a prearranged early hour the following morning. Raycliff then took it the short distance to Bilkin's shop and delivered it.'

'Yes, entirely feasible,' the Colonel agreed. 'I take it then, since the property adjoining Granwell's was the one that had to be destroyed, he set fire to his own place to make sure of getting the property next door?'

'I imagine it was the only course he could take and be sure.' Denning mused for a moment and then went on. 'Granwell claimed he was no chemist — and I believed him, but the more I came to suspect him the more I realized that he could have been lying. I took a chance and went to Somerset House to research into his career from the cradle up, hoping Rupert Granwell was his right name. Evidently it was, for I found him registered as born in Newcastle, his father being a chemist and druggist — I don't need to say more, do I? Where better to learn chemistry tricks than from your own father's business?'

'Nice work,' the Chief Constable commented.

'For a time,' Denning continued, 'I was baffled by his action in destroying his own building. Apart from deflecting suspicion, it had to go in order to destroy the building adjoining and so — with the florist's — complete the triumvirate. It surprised me because it seemed at first that he would not get any insurance money out of it. He told me that he had a complicated policy, a kind of insurance that seemed to cover him against every imaginable thing. He also said that the company was going to pay up.

'I made it my business to find out when he had taken out this 'complete indemnification' policy and discovered it was six months ago. That, no doubt, was the time when he had first decided to embark on arson — and murder too, as it transpired — and at the same time made sure of covering himself financially. Naturally, if we didn't arrest him, he would shortly start buying up all the land, probably through an alias to divert suspicion from himself . . . He won't get away with it.

'One other thing convinced he was back of everything,' Denning resumed after a pause. 'When he came in here and said he had established his claim with the insurance company he had a carnation in his coat. It was the first time I had ever seen him thus adorned, and at the time I didn't think much of it — but later, when Dr. Carruthers explained how somebody had planted iodide of nitrogen outside the florist's, I guessed where the carnation had come from. It had been used as an excuse to enter the shop and so make things look quite normal to Mr. Bedford. Maybe Granwell ordered other flowers; I don't know. Incidentally, early on in the business — when he must have realized that I was finding out far too much for his comfort — Granwell threatened to move heaven and earth to get rid of me if I didn't get results. Evidently he was trying to scare me off . . . '

'In regard to Lloyd,' Colonel Barrow said, 'how did you come to suspect him?'

'He gave himself away all over the place! His worry over the destroyed buildings was not convincing: no Borough Surveyor would worry over that unless he had a big stake in things somewhere.

Further, he told me that he knew a big monopoly would take over the town. He was altogether too wise before the event. I got the impression of a man forced into a corner and for that reason making as clean a breast of everything as he could without — so he hoped — giving himself away. He tried to warn me what would happen to the florist's but there wasn't time to take action. What cinched it for me was the revelation, through his daughter and Gordon Drew, that he is financially embarrassed. That, and the knowledge that murder had been done, would make any man of Lloyd's calibre nervous . . . '

'I knew I wasn't mistaken in your ability, Denning,' the Chief Constable said quietly. 'And now?'

'I'm having warrants issued by a J.P. within the next half-hour and then I'm going to get Granwell for murder and arson, and, regrettably, Lloyd for complicity . . . Yes, come in,' Denning broke off, as the sergeant-in-charge entered.

'Mr. Granwell to see you, sir,' he announced.

Rupert Granwell came in slowly, taking off his hat and putting it on the end of the desk. He merely nodded to the three men and then turned to look at Denning.

'I think you have had fair warning, Superintendent, that I have decided to get you removed from your position as head of the Halingford police. I believe that properties round here — and lives too — are still in danger. I'm on my way now to see the Mayor. He can take the necessary steps to secure your resignation . . . and, Colonel Barrow, it will reflect on you too.'

'Will it really?' the Chief Constable marvelled at the man's sublime impudence.

'I fail to see upon what grounds you assume inactivity on my part, Mr. Granwell,' Denning answered, eyeing him.

'That should be nakedly plain! Three people warned of disaster to come — and you were powerless to prevent it each time!'

'Thanks, Mr. Granwell, for confirming my own suspicions,' Denning smiled.

'Though I never expected you would come right into my office and do it!'

'Suspicions?' Granwell's expression changed abruptly. '*What* suspicions?'

Denning did not answer the question. Instead: 'Tell me one thing, Mr. Granwell. How do you know Mr. Bedford received a warning? It certainly can't be from the newspapers because I had the fact suppressed. So I repeat, how do you know?'

'Because,' Granwell answered smoothly, 'Bedford himself told me he had. I called in his shop to order some flowers for my wife — and get a buttonhole for myself before going to London to see the insurance company.'

'Did Bedford show you the warning?' Denning snapped.

'Of course he did. I read it for myself.'

'Did you really? Bedford couldn't have shown you the warning because he had not even opened the envelope! The only reason you know about it is because you sent it . . . Bedford never reported that he had received warning. I found it on him, unopened, after he died. Those facts won't make very good grounds for having me removed from office, will they? And don't forget that the statement you've just made has been before witnesses.'

Granwell hesitated. Silently the detective-sergeant moved towards the doorway and barred it with his powerful frame.

'You needn't waste your time with excuses, Mr. Granwell,' the Chief Constable observed. 'The game's up — and Denning here has got you on all counts. We know all about the plot to get land by destroying the buildings which stood in the way of the deal, of your scheme to gain eventual monopoly over the town — the nitro-glycerin, the iodide of nitrogen . . . Every detail.'

Granwell stood scowling, lips compressed, for several moments. For some reason he did not look nearly as concerned as he should have done.

'Apparently,' he said, 'I've put my foot in it! I wondered that night after I had sent the warning off to Bedford if it would reach him by the next day. There was no clearance time tablet in the box and I'd posted the note before I noticed the fact. I hoped he might tell me something if he had received the warning: that was why I went in for flowers.'

'And to load up the cactus compost with iodide of nitrogen,' Denning added. 'Your actions would be hidden for the most part by the seed packets which formed a blind across the front door.'

'All right,' Granwell said, with a shrug of his broad shoulders. 'So I gambled and lost. That's the end of it. That's the kind of man I am — and you're a damned sight smarter than I thought, Denning! Not, as you will see shortly, that it will do any of you any good finally.'

Granwell looked about him on the three stern faces and smiled. 'I'm willing to admit defeat — up to a point. However, before you start reciting that charming little piece about arresting me and taking down whatever I have to say in writing, let me make a statement of my own . . .'

Grant moved slightly in his guardianship of the door and picked up his notebook. Granwell's eyes strayed to him, then back to Denning.

'I'm not in this business by myself, you

know,' he said dryly. 'There's the Borough Surveyor also — Geoffrey Lloyd. He's in as deep as I am. Bit of a surprise for you, eh?'

'I said that we know *everything*!' the Chief Constable retorted.

'So you found out about Lloyd too, eh?' Granwell reflected and sighed. 'All right; just thought I'd make sure he gets his share of trouble. And there's that thick-headed oaf of a Billy Greer — the one who polished off Clayton Ross.'

'He calls himself Harry Raycliff,' Denning remarked.

'Take it from me his name's Billy Greer, and though I did give him instructions to find and kill Ross — because I had guessed how much he knew of the truth — it was Greer's hands which did it not mine. He's an ex-wrestler, and I've employed him for quite a long time. After the affair of the nitro-ice I had him lie low in Werton, but on the disappearance of Ross I told him to keep his eyes open as much as possible in case Ross came over righteous and decided to return and say something. I never expected that Greer would have the good luck to spot Ross when he did return, but evidently he did. He did his job ruthlessly, but with an appreciable absence of finesse, which brought about his capture. Can't expect much else of his type.'

'Did you prepare the nitro-glycerin in the dispensary?' Denning asked briefly.

'Yes,' Granwell answered calmly. 'And, if you're wondering about it, I arranged for the Cold Ice truck to be borrowed. I knew Bilkin's actions to the last detail . . .'

'Did you know that Ross had overheard your plans?' Denning asked.

'I assumed as much when I knew he had come to see me at five-thirty on the Monday evening and then had not finished the job. The fact of the warning in advance, to Bilkin, satisfied me that Ross was back of it.'

'And you planted the *Gazette* in the dispensary bin to make it look as though Ross had done it?'

'Yes,' Granwell answered, with suspicious frankness. 'And I expect the matter of the nail scissors which did the job of cutting has been occupying your mind?'

He felt inside his coat and tossed a pair of folding scissors on the desk. Denning looked at them but did not pick them up.

'It amazes me,' the Chief Constable said, 'that two men such as yourself and Geoffrey Lloyd should so debase yourselves for the sake of having an all-powerful business influence.'

'I have a maxim, Colonel. Crush — or be crushed. I received definite wind of the fact that other big combines were thinking up schemes to gain control over this well populated district of Halingford, so I acted first. Had things gone right and I had been able to build up indefinitely — at the same time achieving an impregnable position on the Council — I could have netted a vast fortune from my various stores-to-be. In turn I could have extended elsewhere, ever growing. What upset my plans was Ross's confounded interference in sending a warning first. I had to do the same thing afterwards to try and throw the blame in his direction. But for him I'm pretty sure I would have got away with it . . . Then of course I had reckoned without Dr. Carruthers and his scientific knowledge. Once the thing was launched, though, I was determined to go on.'

'At least your admissions are frank enough,' Denning told him.

'I've nothing to lose because I've no intention of ever going to trial. I'm not that kind of man. I really came here tonight to try and find out, following the announcement in the paper of Greer's arrest, if he had broken down and told everything. I fully expected he would have done, in which case I might be walking into the lion's den. Though I am caught just the same it is apparently not because of him.'

'That dumb bruiser is far more loyal to you than you deserve,' Denning answered.

'Apparently. But for me the answer is the same. I came prepared. I shall not go to trial, gentlemen. In fact none of us will leave this office alive . . . '

Granwell withdrew his hand suddenly from his left overcoat pocket and held up a long thin glass phial with a rubber cork in the top. It contained a curious semi-crystalline substance that caught the electric light in a prismatic glitter.

'I think I have already demonstrated my powers as a chemist,' Granwell remarked coldly. 'This stuff is not anything unusual — nothing as subtle as frozen nitro-glycerin or iodide of nitrogen. It is simply mercury-fulminate, which in case you may not know is one of the most powerful explosives — outside the atomic group — known to science. I have merely to drop it and all that has been said in here — and ourselves — will cease to be of interest to the world in general.'

17

At about the time Rupert Granwell arrived at the police station Dr. Carruthers also had a visitor — and he was not particularly pleased about it. He was conducting some abstruse experiment and was hard at work in his laboratory — Gordon assisting — when the housekeeper announced that Miss Lloyd and her father wished to see him.

'Oh well, all right,' Carruthers said grudgingly, turning from the binocular-microscope with a sigh. 'Show them into the Den; I'll be up right away.' And as the woman went away Carruthers pulled off his overall and eyed Gordon suspiciously. 'Sure you didn't arrange this, son? Because Miss Lloyd would be more interesting than filterable viruses?'

Gordon grinned. 'I didn't arrange anything! I haven't the remotest idea what they can want.'

By the time they had reached the Den

Carruthers' ire at being disturbed seemed to have spent itself and he greeted the grave-looking girl and her father cordially enough as they rose and shook hands.

Carruthers motioned back to the chairs and pulled one up for himself. Gordon hesitated beside the desk. 'If this is to be a private conversation — ' he began.

'No,' Lloyd interrupted, 'I'd much rather you hear everything, Gordon. Your father and I were the closest of friends. And you and Jan being as you are . . . ' The Borough Surveyor hesitated and then turned back to Carruthers' intent face. 'I don't quite know how to begin, Doctor: it's so embarrassing.'

'Then perhaps I can start the ball rolling,' Janice said, with her usual practicality. 'I've been tackling Dad about his being so worried lately, and I finally managed to get the truth out of him. He's worried because he's mixed up in these disasters that have been happening in Halingford.'

'Yes, I'm aware of that,' Carruthers said calmly.

'You — you knew?' Lloyd exclaimed,

frowning. 'But how could you?'

'Merely a matter of inference . . . I'm not, of course, a policeman, thank God, but that doesn't prevent me deducing logical conclusions from given premises. In fact a scientist spends his life doing just that. I have been mixed up in this case more than somewhat, on the scientific side, and have learned most of the things Denning has learned. The fires were started, of course, because three properties blocked the path to property expansion and land-sale.

'Granwell did all the dirty work and presumably roped you in with glowing promises — one, to make you keep your mouth shut, because he guessed you would know who was back of the crimes, and two because your financial embarrassment made it essential you keep your high position. I suppose he offered you vast opportunities in the new Council set-up when, in charge of the legally released land, he would be set up as a tin-pot dictator?'

'That is the situation exactly,' Lloyd admitted quietly. 'But the whole thing has taken such a horrible turn! I agreed with the idea of destroying those three properties — in fact I had hardly any say in it as far as Granwell was concerned — because I didn't see there was any disadvantage in being rid of Bilkin's and of Bedford's ancient properties, but I give you my solemn word that I thought Granwell meant to engineer everything without harm to the occupants. He could have done so with Bedford because he didn't live on the premises. A fire at night could have been arranged.'

'Hardly the way Granwell planned it — with iodide of nitrogen,' Carruthers answered. 'It needed somebody to bump the stuff to start it off. A fire by night, on the other hand, might have left some traces of the 'arrangement' in the ashes. With iodide of nitrogen no trace at all would be left. Likewise, the frozen nitro-glycerin sent to Bilkin left no trace. But for the warnings sent beforehand the three crimes could have been so perfect as to defy detection . . . But go on.'

'I completely underestimated the ruthlessness of Granwell. I felt sure he'd find some way to get the Bilkin family out of the property before destroying it. When he didn't and I knew the horrible thing that had happened, I was appalled. Upon reading of it in the newspaper, I thought that Granwell had sent the warning, then he told me that he hadn't and that he suspected it was the work of Clayton Ross. I had the horrible knowledge that he simply hadn't taken the least precaution to give warning. I was not much worried over the emporium fire because it was Granwell's own concern and nobody was hurt, but when it came to the killing of Bedford and the destruction of his place . . . Well!

'I betrayed my uneasiness before Jan, and finally — to ease my mind — I gave her the details. I wanted to go to the police there and then, but Jan suggested that I see you first. Naturally, you find it hard to believe in my actions?'

'Not entirely,' Carruthers responded. 'Stranger things have happened when one man, utterly ruthless, has dragooned another. It is perfectly clear that you had no other choice. But you've done the right thing now and that is the main point. I think we should walk over and have a word with Denning right away.'

* * *

'So you see, gentlemen, the whole matter is easily settled,' Granwell said, considering the raised phial in his hand. 'There is no harm in making a confession when you know it will never be of any use to anybody.'

The three men shifted their eyes uneasily from Granwell's grim features to the gleam of the deadly mercury-fulminate in his hand. Denning was toying with the idea of a desperate leap forward and only refraining because he knew the slightest of bumps would detonate the stuff. The Chief Constable sat rigid, and the detective-sergeant moved very slightly and then halted again as Granwell looked at him menacingly.

'On the other hand,' Granwell added, 'there is perhaps no point in throwing away my life. Only you three men here know the full facts and with you out of the way it is doubtful if anybody else would be able to pick up the threads. Since explosions are common in Halingford these days one more — in the police station — would probably not be considered unusual . . .

'Yes, that's an interesting thought! I think I'll retire gracefully, gentlemen, and toss you this as a present as I leave. I shall get the blast, of course — but you will get the essence!'

Granwell collected his hat with his free hand and put it on, then he began to back towards the door. Grant moved away from him — but just as Granwell got to the door there were voices in the office outside and not a couple of seconds afterwards a sharp authoritative knock, and the door opened.

'Wait — for God's sake!' Denning shouted hoarsely.

Granwell swung back from the door as it lunged open before the vigorous arrival of Dr. Carruthers. At the same instant Grant dived forward and Granwell threw the phial. In a flying movement Denning fielded it just before it touched the floor. He straightened up with his face looking as though he had lifted it from a bowl of water.

Granwell twisted round and dived for the doorway but Lloyd, Janice, and Gordon Drew blocked his path. He was forced back into the office and Grant kicked the door shut

'What's going on?' Carruthers enquired. 'What are you looking so hot and bothered about Denning . . . Got your man, I see. Took you long enough.'

'This — this phial,' Denning whispered, dry-lipped, staring at it in his hand. 'It's mercury-fulminate. Granwell was going to drop it and blow us sky-high as he escaped.'

Carruthers took the phial and held it to the light. He took out the rubber cork and sniffed at the phial's contents. Finally he put the cork back and tossed the phial in the air. In paralysed horror all, save Granwell and Carruthers, watched it hit the wood floor and splinter. Liquid rolled out turgidly and settled on the wood, leaving gummy, sticky traces.

'Mercury-fulminate my eye,' Carruthers observed sourly. 'Glycerine, and a few drops of mercury to make it look good.

No chemist would walk about with mercury-fulminate in his pocket. A slip on the edge of the kerb, an accidental collision with somebody, and — whoof! A nice little trick, Superintendent, which very nearly got you by the nose.'

'What the devil are you doing here, Lloyd?' Granwell demanded.

'I'm here to give myself up,' Lloyd answered. 'I can't believe though, that you're here for the same reason.'

'I'll be glad to have verification of the things Granwell has had to say,' Denning told the Borough Surveyor. 'What have you to tell me?'

Without hesitation Lloyd began the story he had already told Dr. Carruthers . . .

* * *

It was midnight before every detail — including the charges — had been completed to Denning's satisfaction. Tired but distinctly satisfied, he sat in his office with the Chief Constable, Grant, and Carruthers.

'You've done damned well, Denning,' Colonel Barrow summed up. 'This may mean promotion for you.'

'Thank you sir — but a lot of the credit attaches to Dr. Carruthers here. Without his scientific knowledge I might have struggled.'

Carruthers chuckled. 'As I said, I'm a sort of 'Admirable Crichton' of science. Say no more. What sort of a sentence will Lloyd get?'

'I've no idea,' Denning shrugged. 'Nothing like Granwell's penalty, anyway. Evidently the mercury trick was to give him a chance to make a getaway.'

'I'll throw in what help I can for Lloyd,' the Chief Constable said. 'He's a good friend, but an easy tool for a damnable rogue like Granwell.'

'I'll help you there, Colonel,' Carruthers said. 'I feel it's my duty with young Gordon intending to make a go of it with Janice.'

Denning half smiled and then became serious again. He was thinking of Claire Denbury. The next morning he received a letter from her saying she had decided to avail herself of his suggestion and would be in Halingford within the next few days.

For Denning this was enough. He felt quite confident that his conversations with her would go far beyond the mere outlining of court procedure . . .

THE END

We do hope that you have enjoyed reading this large print book.

Did you know that all of our titles are available for purchase?

We publish a wide range of high quality large print books including:
Romances, Mysteries, Classics
General Fiction
Non Fiction and Westerns

Special interest titles available in large print are:
The Little Oxford Dictionary
Music Book, Song Book
Hymn Book, Service Book

Also available from us courtesy of Oxford University Press:
Young Readers' Dictionary
(large print edition)
Young Readers' Thesaurus
(large print edition)

For further information or a free brochure, please contact us at:

Other titles in the
Linford Mystery Library:

THE WHISTLING SANDS

Ernest Dudley

Along with a large cash legacy, Miss Alice Ames had inherited the Whistling Sands, an old house overlooking the Conway Estuary. And it was here she began married life with Wally Somers — alias Wally Sloane, wanted by the Sydney police. To Wally, Alice and the Whistling Sands were just a means to the money he stood to gain. But when both had come to mean more to him than that, he became enmeshed in a web of deceit — and murder . . .

PLACE MILL

Barbara Softly

In 1645, the Civil War rages and young Nicholas Lambert joins the Royalist Army, leaving his sister Katharine behind. Six years later, with the Royalists defeated, Nicholas is a fugitive. Returning home for safety, accompanied by two friends, he finds much has changed. Taking Katharine and his cousin Hester as cover, they attempt to escape to France, but encounter difficulties before even reaching the coast. And then Katharine disappears . . . Suspicious of their new acquaintances, who will they be able to trust?

DEAD WEIGHT

E.C. Tubb

Sam Falkirk, Captain in the World Police stationed at the World Council in New York, investigates the death of Angelo Augustine, a Council employee. Superficially a parcel courier, Angelo had also spied for Senator Rayburn, whose power-hungry plan is the destruction of the Orient. Meanwhile, Senator Sucamari of the Japanese legation has a deadly plan himself, involving a parcel containing a Buddha coated with enough bacteria to cause a plague across the Americas. When the parcel is stolen can Falkirk find the criminal in time?

ONE FOR THE ROAD

Peter Conway

After a car accident shatters the lives of Mike and Penny Craven, the ex-racing car driver's morale is low. However, when he sees a young woman attacked by thugs and rescues her, his life begins to take on a new meaning. But soon his courage, his skill as a driver and his marriage are all called into question as he and the young woman face violence and death at the hands of a group of vicious criminals.